A Bowl Full of Marbles

Flashes, Sparks, and Shorts. Flash Five

Paul John Hausleben

Cover photographs by Paul John Hausleben

Cover design, and cover concept by Paul John Hausleben

Photographs of the author are by Ms. Cali Rose

Logos, drawings, and images are by Paul John Hausleben

Any scripture references are from: The Holy Bible, King James Version. Cambridge Edition: 1769. Public Domain

Published by God Bless the Keg Publishing LLC

Henrico, Virginia, U.S.A.

ISBN: 979-8-9894490-4-0

Dedication

"For all the marbles"

A Bowl Full of Marbles

Flashes, Sparks, and Shorts. Flash Five

Paul John Hausleben

Contents

Acknowledgements

Thank you, as always, to Mr. Harry M. Rogers Junior. Thank you to my friends and family. Thanks to my dear Mum for the spark right at the end. Many thanks for all the people in my life that must suffer, or have suffered, while listening to my seemingly endless stories and endured my very strange sense of humor. I appreciate your collective efforts at listening, and your support, more than I can properly convey in words.

"There, the snow glistened like diamonds, sleeping until the wind disturbed the piles once more."

Paul John Hausleben

March 2025

Author Notes

I have what I call the PJH story vault. I also have the PJH photograph vault. Now, these are not physical vaults, bolted to the floor like some type of impenetrable safe. They are electronic files in folders on flash drives or on hard drives. The files within those folders contain rejected stories, good stories, very bad stories, or stories that I wrote and decided that I would use them later down the road. Just not right then. When I wrote them. Ditto with the photographs.

Occasionally, I jump into those folders and review them and when the moon is full, and the wind blows out of the northwest, and the stars all align, I find something that catches my eye. Most of the time, I forget why the story or photograph ended up banished to the vault to begin with. Generally, these stories and photos are from a few months ago, or in some cases, many years ago!

Once such story is here, in this collection, and it helps tag along on the cover as a title to the book.

"A Bowl Full of Marbles" is a short story that I wrote a few years earlier for a Christmas collection of stories. It was just a little too long for that collection; hence, it ended up in the vault. Must watch those page counts! They influence the retail prices.

Business. Far too often it gets in the way.

When I revisited the short story, I really enjoyed the characters, the storyline, and the meaning behind the story. It was solid; just needed some touch-up and some slight rewrites. Now, here is the twist and turn of these author notes. In my photographic vault, I found a photograph from about five years earlier of a bowl full of marbles. It was from a photoshoot series that I shot for still photography of common household items. Toys included.

It was a wonderful photograph. I cannot understand or recall why I stuck it in the PJH photography vault! The lighting is great, the glass marbles are very colorful and intricate, and the glass bowl is full of interesting facets and reflections. I put two-and-two together. The photograph can grace the book cover, and the short story can be an anchor story. And then, on a deep dive into the files, Paulie found another quality story in the vault. It was originally going to be a novella featuring the Quiet Stranger in the Black Hat, with a Christmas or winter setting, but for some reason, off that story went to solitary confinement in the vault, too.

When I read that story, I felt it was a quality piece; however, sorry, Quiet Stranger, we love you and no offense, but you need to go back in the vault until next time. We cannot mix our Flashes, Sparks, and Shorts with the mysterious stranger.

At least, not right now. . ..

I was all set now. Two short stories. Now, I simply must write all kinds of other stories and flash fiction pieces and some sparks to fit all around them. You know, the easy part. . .. (wink-wink)

It works for Paulie!

Off I went on a writing tear, and filled in the blanks between the two anchor stories.

On this go-around, in what is now the fifth book in the series of Flashes, Sparks, and Shorts, I included some more content of that PJH off-beat humor to round out the mixture. I sometimes get a bit thoughtful, and deep and dark, and I feel that I need to "jolly" it up a bit and return to my writing roots with some trademark weird Paulie humor.

Herein, I did so.

Occasionally, I revisit those vaults and it is worthwhile for me to do so!

I enjoyed composing this collection of stories and snapping the cover photograph, too! I hope you enjoy reading the stories and viewing the photograph, as much as I enjoyed the experience of creating them!

Thank you!

Paul John Hausleben

March 2025

1

Short

A Bowl Full of Marbles

David Alfred Brown III was a curious little fellow. At eight years of age, he was quite advanced in his reading skills, his mathematics, and his overall school studies. The comment that his teachers always commonly noted was that "David is very intelligent and his mind wanders. As if his studies bore him because he always is looking answers and asking many questions."

The sign of high intelligence is often an inquisitive mind. With questions often come answers; with answers come more questions.

It was Christmas Day in 1972 and the Brown family gathered to enjoy the hope, joy, love, and peace of the graceful and glorious holiday. Little David and his older sister joined in the celebration, too. After opening their presents and enjoying the grandeur and excitement of an early Christmas Day at their own home, it was the stereotypical, "Over the river and through the wood's journey to Grandpa and Grandma Brown's house they go!"

Often the excursion and spending the rest of Christmas Day there, met with some moans and groans; as the youngsters would rather stay put in their own home and enjoy their new toys and gifts and toss the boring socks, tee shirts, and underwear gifts aside. Nevertheless, off to the grandparents, they all dashed. Not in a one-horse open sleigh, but in the family sedan. The 1970s were a simpler time in this world. When family values remained an integral part of life, when religion and God were important and values were paramount. Paramount, in families, in relationships, in actions and demeanor. A visit to the grandparents was on the essential holiday list back then; even if the children moaned and groaned. Years later, they would recall those times for the special moments in life that they were and they are, and they always should be. More than a moment in time, more than just memories. Those moments were simple joy.

And Grandpa Brown decked the halls for the holidays! There were wreaths on the doors, and wax angels and Santa Claus figurines on the fireplace mantle and on the wooden ledge over the arch between the dining room and the living room. There were beautiful lights inside the house and outside the house, and a glorious Christmas tree. And there were mounds of gifts under that same tree. And a small plastic tree with tiny glass ornaments stood proudly on the main dresser upstairs in Grandpa and Grandma's bedroom. Don't touch it now! It is very old and fragile. Grandpa Brown built a glorious roaring fire in the old fireplace to keep everyone cozy and warm and snug. And there was a felt Christmas card holder hung on a door, stuffed full of Christmas cards from family and friends both near and far away. With grand designs and glitter on some of the cards. Glitter that stuck to your fingers and your thumbs and then on the end of your nose and remained there for weeks after touching the cards. No soap is known to remove Christmas card glitter stuck to the end of an eight-year-old's nose. . ..

While an old vacuum tube radio sat on an end table in the living room and the radio played Christmas music from the local radio station, Grandma Brown cooked up a grand feast. There was a twenty-two-pound turkey baking in the oven, filled with stuffing made with a secret family recipe, full of spices and wholesomeness. And there were vegetables; green beans, diced carrots, whipped turnips, mashed potatoes, and homemade turkey gravy! And there were bowls of homemade cranberry sauce, and cakes and pies, and ice cream and a plum pudding. There was fresh apple cider, and beer, and wine, and maybe a shot of whiskey or two for Grandpa Brown and his son and an uncle or two. Christmas cheer! For sure! To warm the soul and loosen the tongue. Not too much now!

And there were memories and love all around.

And there was a bowl full of marbles. . ..

The bowl full of marbles sat on a solid old end table set in a corner of the spare bedroom upstairs. The spare bedroom, where Grandpa Brown sat and watched his baseball games in the summer, and Grandma would sit in an old family rocking chair and knit. She wasn't much of a baseball fan, but she would sit and just enjoy her husband's love of the games.

The bowl was just a plain, clear, glass bowl, with some cut facets of glass from halfway down the bowl to the bottom edge. The bowl filled to the brim with colorful marbles. Some of them were solid colors; red, blue, black, green, purple, and yellow. Others were Cat's Eyes, and were clear glass with swirls and whirls of colors stuck deep inside them. Some were shooters, some were medium, and some were small. The bowl full of marbles sat on an elegant, crocheted, white doily table throw, and it sat mysteriously, yet colorfully, on the old wooden table in the corner of the spare room. The table seemed as if it was ancient; at least a hundred years old or so. Maybe even more. Another Brown family heirloom. From the family roots back in England. Brought here and now, it was a family treasure. In the areas not covered by the doily, the top showed the wear of the years, the finish peeling, and the bare oak wood underneath wore the marks and stains of the years as if they were badges of courage. The legs of the old table had small lines of turnings, not elaborate, and not intricate, just plain, yet appealing and somewhat fashionable. The legs bolted to a sturdy ledge underneath the table and provided a mount and a support. Not that the weight of the marbles was of any great concern; but in the table's many prior lives, it was apparent that it held heavier and more troublesome weights. Despite its age, it was still very capable of doing so.

When the family finished the Christmas feast; it was time to relax! The dishes were clean and tucked away in the cupboards, and the desserts served, all the bellies full, and the grown-ups all gathered around the fireplace and shared stories of lore and old and some new. All while sipping hot and cold beverages. Some beverages were stronger in content than others were. . ..

They had to watch old Uncle Bernie. He tended to dive deep into the Christmas cheer every year. Once into the Christmas cheer, he even did the backstroke.

Underneath the Christmas tree, the children sat and played with new found joy and listened to the stories and the laughter and the sharing of joy between the grown-ups and the family.

While his sister and cousins played, little David wandered. Not that David did not love and cherish his new Christmas gifts; especially the new hat for his favorite hockey club, and the Bernie Parent poster, and the other gifts from his grandparents, but his mind tuned into the inquisitive band. It was time to check everything out; make new memories, discover new avenues, and take a snapshot of them and stick them in his mind's eye. David found his wanderings taking him to the upstairs spare room. To the family photographs on the walls. To the old-fashioned wallpaper with lilies and colors and some peeling seams that Grandpa Brown will fix in the spring. To the steam cast-iron radiator with a stainless-steel pan of water set on the cover; a pan to add some moisture to the dry winter air. To the old television set on a wooden cart in the corner of the room. The spare television in the spare room. Eventually, David's fascination and focus landed on the bowl full of marbles. On the old table. On the white crotched doily. To the meaning of it. To the beautiful and varied colors. His mind wandered as to what exactly was the meaning of the bowl full of marbles. Or was there any meaning at all? Was it just beautiful to look at? Or did Grandpa and Grandma play marbles? He thought they seemed too old for those sorts of games.

Grandpa Brown was always in tune with all his grandchildren and he loved them all equally. At this point in his life; they were his joy. Along with his wife of fifty years! He was tall, slightly bent from age now at the waist, with a wisp of white hair that glided over the top of his head. His smile was quick, his proneness to laughter even quicker; his dimples were deep and his brown eyes glowed with kindness. They were, in fact, as if they were marbles of glass. Clear and bright.

Yes! He loved all his grandchildren deeply and all his family, too! But "Little David," as the family lovingly nicknamed him, sparked a special flame in his heart. He was the youngest of the crew; and he reminded his grandfather of himself at that same age. Always poking around; restless for adventure and yearning for knowledge, and curious as to the world and the meaning of it all. His grandson had the traits that his grandfather admired and loved, and was all too familiar with.

Out of the corner of his eye, he watched his grandson

wander away from the bright lights and beauty of the Christmas tree, from his sister, and his cousins, and from the gathering, to head upstairs. He knew that it was not to use the bathroom on the second floor. Grandpa Brown recognized that lick in his grandson's eye. It was time to go exploring and his grandfather was interested as to what the mission was that Little David had in mind. Grandpa Brown excused himself from the circle of family and the cheer, and the stories, and he climbed up the long wooden hill to share more time, more holiday joy, and make some more memories with his grandson.

Grandpa Brown found Little David in the spare room, carefully studying the bowl full of marbles.

"Grandpa, I always wanted to ask you. I guess now that I am older, you will tell me. What are these marbles for? In this bowl. They are very cool. I love the colors. I know not to touch stuff. Unless, I ask first. I do not think that you play marbles with Grandma. Do you? Some of the guys at school play marbles. They draw a circle in the dirt in the schoolyard and shoot them around."

Grandpa Brown smiled, and he bent down and kneeled next to his little grandson.

Is there anything in this world more precious than a curious little child is? The world is wide open. The world is an open palate of which to paint excitement on and study and enjoy. They are wide-eyed at it all; at the wonder, and the learning, and the fascination. Especially so at Christmastime. Grandpa Brown's knees cracked as he settled in next to his grandson and he grunted a bit and wrapped his arm around the little boy's shoulders.

"No. I do not play marbles. I used to when I was a little boy. But no longer. That bowl full of marbles is how I track my decisions, Little David. How I track the good choices that I made in life, each day, every day, and how I track the poor ones, too. It is my reminder to make good choices in life and when I do not make a good choice, it helps me to think harder and longer to try to make better choices and to choose more wisely in the future."

David turned to his grandfather, screwed up his little nose and asked, "Huh? Choices? I don't get it, Grandpa Brown. Please tell me."

Grandpa Brown nodded and smiled. He realized as intelligent as the little boy was, he was only eight years old. Lots of life to live. Many more experiences to encounter. Life.

"Ha! I get it, Little David. A little too complicated. My fault. Let me try this. You are a hockey goalie, and a good one, too. So, the shooter is skating in on you. Now, you need to make a choice. Do you drop down to the ice, cover the bottom of the net or do stand up on your skates and take on the shot and make the save? That in life is what we call a decision. A challenge. A choice. Do you do your homework right away, or do you wait until the last minute? Do you pick out chocolate ice cream or vanilla? Or maybe half and half? A little taste of each flavor. Choices. Decisions."

Little David signaled his understanding.

"I get it, Grandpa Brown. I usually stand up on my skates. Make the net small. That is what Coach Ray says I should always try to do. And he was a goalie, too. Always do your homework first. Otherwise, you blow it and never do it. And you get a bad grade. Like an F. It is always vanilla for me. I like vanilla pudding better than vanilla ice cream. I tell my mother that all the time, but she still gives me the ice cream. So, what does that have to do with these marbles?"

"I will see what I can do with your mom about the pudding. Here. Please. Let me show you. When I must make a choice on anything that is important in my life, or now that I am old, almost any choice, then I take a marble out of the bowl and I think long and hard about making the best choice that I can."

Grandpa Brown studied the collection of marbles for a few seconds, and he reached in and plucked a marble with green and yellow swirls inside the glass out of the bowl and he held it in the closed palm of his hand. He continued to explain as his grandson watched and listened.

"Then I walk over here to my end table here and I open up this drawer."

Grandpa Brown walked over to the table that stood next to his easy chair in the same room. Where he watched his baseball games from and relaxed while doing so. Grandpa Brown opened the drawer in that table and plucked a small brown burlap bag out of the drawer. The bag had two cloth drawstrings sewn inside the opening, and Grandpa Brown tugged at the opening to pry the mouth of the bag up.

He then continued to explain.

"I drop the marble in the bag. Close it up and place it back in the drawer. Sometimes, I have to make many choices and I have quite a few marbles in this brown bag. Each marble represents a choice."

Little David leaned in with fascination at the words and explanation of his grandfather. And at the bowl full of marbles and the brown burlap bag. His curiosity piqued.

"When the result of the choice that I made arrives, maybe it is right away, maybe it is a day or two, or a week or maybe even more away, then if I made a good choice, I get the brown burlap bag out, take a marble out and drop the marble back in the bowl. If I made a bad choice. . .."

Grandpa Brown shook his head and he feigned a very sad face, while he continued to explain.

"Then the marbles have to stay in the bag, until I make good choices to put them back in the bowl. Usually, those choices just come along in life. You don't have too much time to think about them, or grab a marble and decide, you just make the decision that you have to at the time. It is a big word. Spontaneous. Like making a save as a goalie. You just do it. That is the way it goes."

Little David's fascination reached its maximum level. He waved to his grandfather to show him the contents of the bag, and Grandpa Brown did so. He leaned over and showed him that the bag only had a few marbles in the bottom of it. Maybe three or four at the most.

"I get it, Grandpa Brown! You don't want to run out of marbles in the bowl!" Little David pointed at the bag and asked, "What choices were those marbles for?"

Grandpa Brown smiled at the little boy's comprehension of the representation of the marbles.

"Yes, exactly. Never run out of marbles, my dear David. Never! Always make keen choices, and when you do not do so, then be sure to correct your ways! Those marbles were for the Christmas present choices that we bought and made for you, your sister, and for your cousins, Greg, and Daisy. The gifts all seem to be winners, so I think that old Grandpa Brown will take three of these marbles out of the bag and drop them back into the bowl. And this one . . . this one stays in the bag. I need to check with Grandma first before deciding where this marble belongs. I am not sure that the dinner rolls that I picked up at the market for Christmas dinner were winners or not."

"Oh, I loved the dinner rolls, Grandpa. Honey and butter on them. Yummy! Winners! That marble can go in the bowl now, too. I know Grandma is happy! We love those dinner rolls. And I know you are right about the other marbles. We all loved our Christmas stuff! I know that my sister loved her curling iron for her fancy hair and my cousins loved their gifts, too! And so were my presents! My hat is super cool. The poster is, too. I will put it on my bedroom wall when we get home. I love Bernie Parent! The best goalie ever. I want to be just like him!"

Grandpa Brown threw back his head and began laughing. It was a good laugh. A laugh full of joy. He wrapped his arm around his grandson and gently guided the little boy back to the table with the bowl full of marbles.

"Yes! Every hockey fan loves Bernie! Even if you do not root for the Flyers! How could you not? Only the Lord saves more than Bernie Parent! Every goalie wants to be Bernie!"

Grandpa Brown poured the marbles from the bag into the bowl and he dropped the marble representing the dinner roll choice into the bowl, too.

"There you go, Little David. Almost filled back up again!"

"I love this! It teaches you math, too! Kind of. I don't like math, Grandpa Brown, but my teacher says I have to do it and be good at it, too. How do you know how to keep track of them all?"

Grandpa Brown bent down again and his knees cracked once more. Loudly.

He wrapped his left arm around his grandson and, with his right hand, he playfully tapped his forehead and said, "Oh, you will know. You will know, Little David."

Little David was very smart and inquisitive. He knew all the proper questions to ask.

"What if you make all bad choices and run out of marbles? What do you do then? Have you ever run out, Grandpa Brown?"

"Well, no. I never have run out of marbles in the bowl. Came close a few times, but like a good goalie does, I made a few saves right at the end of the game to win and pulled it out just before the marbles ran out. When you make a few good choices, then you can put some marbles back in the bowl. Eventually, it teaches you to get smarter and the bowl fills back up once more."

Grandpa Brown turned and pointed at the bowl full of marbles. He then continued to teach and explain to his grandson, his wisdom, his thoughts, and his simple method of tracking his own life.

"Remember David, every day, you make choices. You face many decisions. Countless. Immeasurable. Right from wrong. Wrong from right. Easy and hard. Simple and complicated. Right now, as a little boy . . . they are easier choices. Such as doing your homework, studying for a test, or playing hockey with your buddies, doing your chores now, or waiting until later, listening to your teachers, practicing your goalie exercises, or being lazy. Easy. As you grow up, the choices become more and more difficult. What job to take? What woman to love? Whether to buy that house or not. Or a new car? Or a used one? Right from wrong? Wrong decisions from right decisions? In an entire lifetime, there are so many decisions to make. Perhaps too many. Pray about them all. Choose wisely. The marbles are simply a way to track your successes and your failures. Allow your heart to guide your decisions and you will not fail and the bowl will remain full. Try your best never to lose the marbles. You will gain them. You will lose them. We are only human. We make dumb-dumb mistakes. The trick is never to let all the marbles run out."

Little David looked up at his grandfather and then back to the bowl full of marbles.

The little boy nodded and said, "I understand, Grandpa

Brown. I do."

Grandpa Brown smiled and said, "Good. When you are young, it is easy, then it grows more and more difficult, and now, when you are very old, like I am, and most of the difficult choices in life are over and done with, it is easy. Dinner rolls! Gifts! Should I have another beer? Should I stay up late and watch the baseball game? Easier choices. But life is hard. When you are little, you have little troubles. When you are big, you have big troubles. Do your best. Every single day. Always do your best."

Grandpa Brown reached over and he hugged his precious grandson and fought back the tears. This boy was special. He knew that. The little boy hugged his grandfather. Absorbed his wisdom and his warmth.

Little David whispered, "I love you, Grandpa. Thank you."

Grandpa Brown whispered back, "I love you, too. Merry Christmas."

"Merry Christmas, Grandpa."

Grandpa Brown's eyes flickered as he said, "Now, about that pudding. . .."

Grandpa Brown had very kind eyes.

Every day, in our lifetimes, we all face choices and decisions. Hundreds, maybe a thousand. Who knows how many?

A bowl full of marbles.

It was Christmas Day in 1974. The Brown family gathered once more at Grandpa and Grandma Brown's home for another glorious Christmas Day celebration. Once more, yes, the Brown family gathered to enjoy the hope, joy, love, and peace of the graceful and glorious holiday. Now, Little David teetered upon not actually being "Little David" any longer. He was now ten-years of age and a few months more, and he was already growing taller, and leaner, and stronger, and losing his baby face and baby body. On the edge of growing into a teenager. Yet, not quite there. Still innocent, and intelligent, and keen, and as inquisitive as ever. Perhaps even more so than he previously was. Off they went; over the river and through the woods. . ..

After opening the gifts from their grandparents, the children of the Brown family sat on the floor of the living room and played with and admired their new Christmas gifts. There were board games, and a few toy trucks, some plastic soldiers, and a doll or two. Along with candy, some money for their piggy banks, and some novelty gifts, too! And of course, "the boring" gifts of socks and hats, and underwear.

Grandpa Brown cruised through the living room to check on the kiddies and when he did so, he gently touched Little David on the shoulder and gave him a wink and then a wave. He wanted Little David to follow him. Up the long wooden staircase, they went.

To the upstairs bedrooms and as they climbed, Grandpa Brown asked Little David, "Did you check out the little plastic Christmas tree in Grandpa and Grandma's bedroom this Christmas? I know you usually wander and you enjoy that little tree."

"I do, Grandpa Brown! I do! I love that little tree. It is very cool. I was going to come up and check it out. Just got busy."

"Well, let's look together now. Before we all sit down for our Christmas feast. Shall we?"

They entered the bedroom and there the little plastic tree sat on the dresser, as it did every Christmas. Old and fragile and nostalgic. Carrying a few lifetimes of Christmas stories and memories along with it. This time, though, there was a large box sitting alongside the little tree. A box, gaily wrapped in Christmas wrapping paper. Grandpa Brown wrapped his arm around his grandson as he pointed at the little tree.

He smiled and said, "It looks as if there is a Christmas present sitting there. Next to the little tree. Usually, there are no presents underneath that tree. I wonder who the present is for and why it is there this Christmas? What do you say? Should we check it out?"

Little David sensed some excitement here. Perhaps the gift was for him! He furiously nodded and dashed off to stand next to the dresser and check out the gift.

"Go ahead, Little David. See who the gift is for."

Little David excitedly picked the gift off the top of the dresser and read the gift tag aloud, "To David A. Brown, the third. From Grandpa and Grandma Brown! It's for me! Can I open it now?"

Grandpa Brown wandered over to the bed, and he sat on the mattress and waved and nodded.

As he sat on the mattress and looked over at his grandson, Grandpa Brown said, "Go ahead. Please do. I told Grandma that we were going to open it now. She will be up here in short order to watch. Ah yes! I hear her steps on the staircase now."

Sure enough, Grandma Brown appeared around the corner. A blue apron around her waist, a smile on her face; her brown eyes sparkling with kindness. She took a break from the dinner preparation to watch the gift unwrapping ceremony. She sat down next to her husband and kissed his cheek.

Then she turned to her grandson and said, "Please. Go ahead, Little David. Open the gift."

Both Grandma and Grandpa Brown had very kind eyes.

As Little David grabbed the gift and began to study how to open it, Grandpa Brown explained, "We gave just a little extra money to your sister and to your cousins, then we did give to you. Because you are receiving this extra gift. We try to be fair to all our grandchildren. But this gift, we think it is kind of special."

When you are ten years old, then Christmas can be very special. Full of wide-eyed exuberance. So far, this Christmas was a very special one; and it was about to become monumental in the life of young David A. Brown III. Little David sat on the floor with the gift box next to him. He caught a corner of the paper and he tore into the wrapping paper as his grandparents sat on the mattress and savored every moment. In short order, the little boy lifted the flaps of the box and stuck his hands down inside of it and felt around. First, he lifted some bubble wrap and from it, he removed a glass bowl. With clear glass and some facets halfway. It looked very familiar!

"A bowl! It is like your bowl. For your marbles!"

He set that aside on the floor. Then from the box, after further probing, he found a bag. A bag full of colorful marbles!

He lifted the bag in the air, smiled and shouted, "I think that I know this gift!" He was quite excited at the prediction.

"A bag of marbles! Cool!" Some of them were solid colors; red, blue, black, green, purple, and yellow. Others were Cat's Eyes, and were clear glass with swirls and whirls of colors stuck deep inside them. Some were shooters, some were medium, and some were small.

"Be sure to poke around inside the box, Little David," Grandma Brown said. "There are a few more items inside there."

The youngster dove his hands inside the maze of crumbled paper and felt around. Sure enough, he pulled out a crocheted white doily, not unlike the one Grandpa Brown had underneath his bowl full of marble. Little David held the doily up and showed his grandparents and stated, "I bet you made this, Grandma. I bet you did."

"I did. I crocheted it for you. Just like the one I made so long ago for your grandpa. There is one more item in the box. Dig around. Don't miss it," she advised.

The final item out of the box was a small brown burlap bag. To place the marbles in until a decision arrived. Little David knew the drill! It was his own bowl full of marbles.

Grandpa Brown advised, "You will need to find a table for your bowl full of marbles. Maybe your father has one you can use or your mother has something in the attic. When I am off and gone, then you can use my table. But for now, we will keep that one in the spare room."

"I'll find a table, Grandpa! And you are not going anywhere! Not in forever!"

He placed the gifts back into the box, jumped to his feet and first he hugged his grandmother, then his grandfather.

"Thank you! The coolest Christmas present ever. Since Jesus got all his stuff! I am going to make all the best choices now!"

Little David's grandparents hugged him back and all together they shared each other's love and warmth. Christmas joy! There is nothing like it!

Grandma Brown said, "You are welcome, David. I must

be back to the dinner now. You two enjoy and hurry on down soon. Dinner is almost ready!"

Little David shouted with continued exuberance, "We will be down soon! Can't wait to eat all the dinner rolls! With butter and honey. This is the best Christmas ever! Now I too, can make the best choices with my own bowl full of marbles! Can we go look at yours, Grandpa? Will you tell me what the decisions are for today?"

"Sure. C'mon over here. Let's check them out together," Grandpa Brown said as he leaned into his grandson. In a low voice, just above a whisper, he said, "You had better leave some of those dinner rolls for me, too."

"I will, Grandpa Brown! I promise!"

Into the spare room they went and Little David immediately ran over to the bowl full of marbles sitting on the old table. He made a careful study of it as his grandfather watched and observed his reactions.

Little David asked, "It is almost full. How many are in your brown bag?"

"Let's take a look, and find out," Grandpa Brown replied as he walked over to the end table, opened the drawer, and removed the brown burlap bag.

"Here you go, Little David. Check and see."

The curious little boy nodded. He took the bag, opened it by the drawstrings and peered inside.

"You only have two marbles in here. Waiting for how your choices turn out. What are they for, Grandpa Brown?"

"Well, one is for whether we should let Uncle Bernie have one glass of my famous Grandpa Brown's eggnog or not. I decided to make my famous eggnog again this year, despite what happened last Christmas with Uncle Bernie."

Little David nodded and recalled the incident. "Oh,

yeah. When he had about ten glasses and fell asleep underneath the Christmas tree and snored so loud that no one could talk or hear the Christmas music. Yup. That marble is going to stay for a while in the burlap bag, Grandpa. He will drink too much eggnog again and the same thing will happen."

Grandpa Brown frowned. He knew that his grandson was very smart, and he was probably correct in his prediction. "I fear you are correct. Oh well, I made the decision and now I will have to plan better."

Little David made a keen observation. "Maybe Uncle Bernie needs a bowl full of marbles to help him to decide how much eggnog to drink!"

Grandpa Brown chuckled and said, "He sure does . . . I am not sure that his marbles would last more than one day until they ran out, but it is a good thought, Little David."

"What is the other marble for?"

"That one is going to be a fun one. When everyone has left tonight and the house is all quiet and the only lights in the house are the lights on the Christmas tree and the candles in the windows, I plan to give your grandma an extra special gift. No, don't tell her! It is a surprise!"

Little David shook his head and crossed his fingers in front of his grandfather as proof of his silence, while he exclaimed, "I won't tell! I promise! A Christmas surprise! What is the special gift?"

Grandpa Brown walked over to Little David and put his arm around his shoulders. He no longer had to bend down to do it, either. Little David had grown up and become David. He was growing like a weed in May.

"It is a necklace. A silver heart locket and inside is a picture. Our favorite wedding picture of us together at our wedding. In January, we will be married for sixty-two years. The picture is a miniature. I had the jeweler assemble it and engrave it with our initials and the date of our wedding. I hope that she likes it! It cost quite a bit of money."

Little David pointed at the marble. He waved in confidence and said, "Oh, yeah. That one is a winner. Great choice, Grandpa. She will love it. You can toss that marble back in the bowl full of marbles now!"

His confidence and actions induced another chuckle from Grandpa Brown, and his kind eyes flickered.

"I hope you are correct, Little David. Then, after she opens the silver locket, I will put it around her neck, put our favorite Christmas song on the record player and we will dance in the living room, right there, in front of the Christmas tree. And then I will kiss your grandma."

"That is nice. Even the kissing part. What is your favorite Christmas song, Grandpa Brown?"

"I'll be home for Christmas. Because when I was away in the military and overseas, I missed four Christmases with your grandma. At the time, we had your father and your Auntie Lisa. Little tikes and I was away for the holidays. We used to play that song all the time. Even in the spring of the year. Whenever, I did have a chance to call your grandma, I would sing it to her and she would sing it to me over the telephone. Now, I am always home for Christmas and until the good Lord takes us to Heaven, we will always be home together. And when we are in Heaven, we will really be home and together forever." Little David reached around his grandfather and they shared a hug. The little boy made another keen observation as they hugged.

"That marble might be the best one ever."

Grandpa Brown hid a tear from his grandson and the words were a little choked, but he managed to say, "I do think it is. I do think that you are correct. The best marble ever."

And later than same Christmas evening, after waking up Uncle Bernie from underneath the Christmas tree and sending him safely home, when all the family left for their own homes, and their own lights, and songs, and love, and maybe even a few dances of their own, Grandpa and Grandma Brown danced in their living room. The only lights in the house were the candles in the windows and the lights from the Christmas tree. The old song played and promised to be home for Christmas once again . . . tonight and forever.

Shortly after the clock struck midnight and Christmas Day turned into Boxing Day, Grandpa Brown turned the light on in the spare room. He shuffled over to grab the brown bag from the drawer. He dropped two marbles from the brown burlap bag back into the bowl full of marbles. One for the silver locket and one for the gift to his grandson, which forgave his eggnog mishap.

He smiled and turned out the light.

Another year; another Christmas Day and a bowl full of marbles.

It was shortly after the big July 4th holiday in 1980. Little David was now simply David. Tall and strong and muscular. Still playing hockey, playing baseball, a hint of whiskers on his chin, on the cusp of manhood. His coaches and managers all said that he was a better goalie than a baseball player, but he was still a fine baseball player. He pitched and played centerfield and could even switch hit fairly well. Baseball was his grandfather's favorite sport.

David was a handsome lad, with a full head of wavy

black hair, solid cheekbones, and a strong chin. Not too prominent; just right. His features were hints of all his relatives; his father, his mother, his grandparents; even good old Uncle Bernie.

All the young ladies gave him a wink and notice.

David sat alone on the edge of his bed in his bedroom and he dried his tears. David had heard his father's footsteps on the staircase and he did not want to show weepy eyes to his father. His mother had great concern for her son and she sent his father on a mission to check on their son. The funeral had been very difficult for him. The knock on the bedroom door was his father's knock.

He rapped a little harder and louder than his mother did. "Come in, Dad," David said.

The door opened slowly and into the bedroom walked David A. Brown II.

He smiled a weak smile and waved at the bed and said, "You knew it was me, huh? Can I sit?"

"Yeah. You knock harder than Mom does. Sure. I will scoot over a bit."

David moved more to the head of the bed and his father sat on the end. David A. Brown II let his eyes wander around the bedroom until they settled on the bowl full of marbles.

He smiled and pointed at the bowl and said, "The old table looks swell there. Sturdy. Grandpa wanted you to have it. He made sure that I promised to fetch it and bring it over as soon as he . . . well . . . passed."

David's bowl full of marbles sat on an elegant, crocheted, white doily table throw, and it sat mysteriously, yet colorfully, on the old wooden table in the corner of David's bedroom. The table seemed as if it was ancient; at least a hundred years old or so. Maybe even more. Another

Brown family heirloom. From the family roots back in England. Brought here and now, carefully preserved. In the areas not covered by the doily, the top showed the wear of the years, the finish peeling, and the bare oak wood underneath wore the marks and stains of the years as if they were badges of courage. The legs of the old table had small lines of turnings, not elaborate, and not intricate, just plain, yet appealing and somewhat fashionable. The legs bolted to a sturdy ledge underneath the table and provided a mount and a support. Not that the weight of the marbles was of any great concern; but in the table's many prior lives, it was apparent that it held heavier and more troublesome weights and, despite its age, it was still very capable of doing so. And now, the table moved to another new home on its long journey. Another life, another phase, a new era.

"Yeah. Thank you. It looks good there. How come you never did the marbles, Dad? How come Grandpa Brown never gave you a Christmas gift like mine? A bowl full of marbles."

David's father pondered the question for a few seconds and then, with a slight shake of his head, he answered.

"I am not exactly sure. My father had keen insight into everyone. I swear my mother and he could look into people's hearts and see so much. If I had to guess, it was because he felt that I would not stick with it. I tended to jump around a lot from one shiny thing, to the next shiny thing, when I was young. Like you, when I was very young, I played hockey and gave it up, even though I was a very good center iceman. Ha! You are a goalie. I never wanted to be a goalie! Those pucks hurt. Then I jumped into baseball, and then basketball. Never stuck with any of them for too long. Then I went to college for one year and gave that up, too. Joined the military. And after that, I became a plumber. I would have run out of marbles in ten minutes. You are more thoughtful than I ever was."

David nodded and his eyes landed on the bowl full of marbles. His eyes welled up with tears.

"Hey, are you okay? I know it is tough. It is part of life, son. A difficult part, but part of life. We all face it." The father scooted over and put his arm around his son, and they remained quiet for a few minutes. "First, Grandma left in the spring and now Grandpa. I get it. I miss them, too. But you are strong. They were with us for so long. Their love and wisdom never will leave us. Ever."

"I am okay. I know that they will never leave us, Dad. It is hard. Very hard. Christmas will never feel the same."

"Oh, I don't know about that. You will marry. Have your own children. Have grand Christmas celebrations. Make choices. And maybe, just maybe, someday, teach one of your own grandchildren about the bowl full of marbles. Besides, Uncle Bernie will still come over, drink too much, and fall asleep underneath the Christmas tree."

David dried his tears and laughed. His father also dried his own tears and shared in the laughter. They both stared at the bowl full of marbles.

"Good old, Uncle Bernie. He will live forever. He sure loves Christmas cheer, Dad."

"He does. It sure seems as if he will be around forever. I think all that cheer preserves and pickles him now." David's father pointed to his son's hand. David held two marbles in his palm and his brown bag sat on the bed next to him.

"Say, what are the two marbles for there? If I might ask and it is not private?"

"Well, one is to decide on showing tears at the funeral. I decided not to cry, so that was a loser and will stay in the bag for a while, until I come up with a good choice. The other one, well, I keep changing my mind on. Should I forget about it and put it back in the bowl, or go for it and put in the brown bag. Been thinking about it for a week or so. Before Grandpa Brown died."

David's father seemed surprised at the time frame.

He asked, "One week ago, and no final decision, huh?"

"Well, it is for whether I should ask Janie Perkins out for the summer dance at church. It is still two weeks away. So, my marble is going in the brown bag now. Right before you came up here, I decided to ask her, but have not asked her yet. Too shaky in my knees."

"Ah yes, knee shake. It happens to all of us men. Even when you are not a teenager. Your mother still makes my knees shake. Do it. Ask her out. She is a pretty gal. From a very good family. Great smile. That one is a winner. She will say yes. I see her stare at you all the time in church and afterwards at the family fellowship hour. Besides, isn't she a hockey fan?"

David nodded and said, "Claims to be. She comes to all my games. But when I ask her to explain icing, she does not understand the rule!"

David's father threw his head back and laughed.

After recovering, he leaned in and said, "I am not sure that I even know what icing is these days. You have my assurances that Janie is not there for the hockey game . . . she is there to watch you, David. Good choice. I bet that marble goes right back in the bowl. Ditch the shaky knees. You are a fearless goalie staring down slap shots from the point. Surely, asking out a pretty gal is not too scary. And David, it is going to be okay. Time will help heal our hearts. Remember, Grandma and Grandpa will always be with us."

He hugged his son, stood up and smiled and headed for

the door.

"Dinner is almost ready. Come on down. Your mother is worried about you."

"Okay, Dad. I will be down in a minute. Thanks for the pep talk. Thanks for everything."

"Of course. I love you."

"Love you too, Dad."

When the door closed and his father left the bedroom, David picked up his brown bag and dropped the two marbles inside and opened a drawer to his dress or and set the bag inside the drawer. Time will tell how it goes. One defeat, hope for a win.

With a sigh, and one more wipe at his eyes, David left the room, and he closed off the light as he did so. The bowl full of marbles sat there glowing with colors and joy even in the darkness. Waiting for the choices.

Waiting for life to evolve. One phase ended, and another begins. The circle of life. Joyous and sad. Difficult and easy. Ebbs and flows.

One week later, David stood next to his bowl full of marbles with a huge smile on his face. He took the two marbles out of the bag and happily dropped them back into the bowl. His first date with Janie Perkins had been a blast. They went to the summer dance and even shared a kiss on the way home. One marble for the choice of asking her out on the date. The other marble because of that amazing kiss. A spontaneous kiss.

His first kiss.

Hers, too.

David Alfred Brown III was a curious and intelligent young man. His teachers and his hockey coach all told him that he was underachieving. Not fully applying himself. So did his dear Janie. His one true love. David sat on the edge of his bed and stared at the bowl full of marbles. There were only three sad, lonely marbles left in the bowl.

It was fall of 1982 and hockey season just started, and much to his dismay, David found that his recent decisions and his spontaneous choices, all went astray.

Hence the lack of marbles.

"I think David needs you, honey," Mrs. Vivian Brown said, as her husband set his lunch pail on the little table in the kitchen. She wiped her hands on her apron, walked over, and gave her husband a kiss on his cheek.

"Welcome home. You look tired. I love you. When I dusted his room this morning, I noticed that his bowl full of marbles was almost empty. He came home from hockey practice and went straight to his room. I asked him what was wrong, and he shook his head and said, 'That he did not want to talk about it.'"

She studied her husband's eyes. He inherited his kind eyes from his parents.

"I love you, too. Yes. Long day. Again. Okay, babe. I will go see what is up. Thank you."

"Dinner is almost ready. If needed, I will keep it warm."

David Alfred Brown II set foot on the first step of the staircase. His steps were distinctive, and in the upstairs bedroom, his son knew the sounds of his father's steps. Very, very well. His father climbed the staircase slower than he did in past years; a lifetime of plumbing work bent him at the waist and put a perpetual set of rather persistent aches in his legs. It took his father longer to arrive at the top of the staircase, but arrive he did.

David Alfred Brown III did not wait for his father to arrive at his bedroom door; instead, he stood up from his bed, walked over to the door, unlocked the button on the door knob, and opened the door wide. He then returned to the edge of the bed and his staring at the bowl; a bowl, not exactly full of marbles. The bowl only had three marbles left in it. He welcomed this visit from his father; he needed his words of wisdom, his love, his guidance. David looked up at his father and smiled a weak smile as his father appeared in the doorway and smiled in return.

He waved at the bed and asked, "Got room for your old man?"

David A. Brown III nodded, patted the bed mattress next to him, and scooted his backside over to make room for his father to sit.

When his father sat, he pointed at the nearly empty bowl of marbles and asked, "So, why the nearly empty bowl? Seems as if you hit a rocky road of sort. Bad decisions?"

"Ah yeah! Lots and lots! I am a total screw-up as of late. And I can't seem to get it right, Dad. Everything and every choice that I do is wrong."

"Okay, well, let's hear it. It might not be as bad as you are saying. I am sure it is not everything. . .."

His voice trailed off and the wise father decided to enter some reality into the conversation and as he pointed at the bowl once more, he added, "Well, it does seem as if nearly every decision as of late went astray. But there is always hope. You do have three left."

"I do. Well, I skipped two hockey practices to hang out with Jerry and the guys. Coach Ray benched me for the scrimmage this Saturday and then he told me, after practice today, that I was second-string to Ruppert. Ruppert stinks. He can't stop a beach ball."

David's father nodded but did not say a word; instead, he waved in the air to hear more.

"Flagged a history exam that I should have aced because. . .."

His father interrupted his son's testimony with a prediction.

"You decided to hang out with Jerry and the guys instead of studying and paying attention."

"Yes. And Janie is really mad at me because she knows that I keep screwing up and she does not like me hanging out with Jerry, and George, and Willy. She says they are a bad influence on me. She said, there are rumors going around in school about Janie and me. And today, after she yelled at me about a bunch of things, she told me that she doesn't want to speak to me for a few days. Says she is thinking about our relationship and where we are together. So, right for now, Janie won't speak to me."

"Oh boy. I see why the bowl is nearly empty. Let me guess. A bunch of other bad choices made on the fly out there. You steal some beers from Jerry's old man from the fridge in his garage and smoke some cigarettes and waste your time. And brag about things you do with your girlfriends. Unsavory things. And because this group of guys are not the most upstanding young men, word got back to Janie 'bout you saying stuff that is not exactly true. Because you wanted to be just like the guys."

David's head snapped around and he stared into his father's kind eyes. He saw those same eyes when he was a little boy. His grandparents had kindness in their eyes, too.

"Exactly. How did you know all of that, Dad?"

David's father smiled widely, threw his head back and laughed and said, "Ha! Because I was not always this old. Look, son, you are eighteen now. A senior in high school.

All kinds of conflicts in your heart. Temptations. Desires. Life choices. A potential college scholarship in hockey waiting for you. A beautiful girlfriend, who you love and make no mistake, she loves you, too. You are now on the edge of manhood. Perhaps you are already a man. You will learn that you are going to make many mistakes. Hence, the bowl of marbles. It is very simple. Grandpa Brown taught you, predicted all of this, lent to you some of his wisdom and a representation of what bad decisions in life mean. Yet, as I just said, there are three marbles left. The game is not over. Still time to make the save and pull it out in the end. Besides, you do not want to end up like Uncle Bernie and fall asleep underneath the Christmas tree every year. Now, what are you going to do with those last three marbles? Because you need to make them count."

David nodded, and he stood up. With confidence and determination, he walked over to the bowl and plucked the last three marbles out and held them in his hand. David clutched them tightly for a few moments and then opened his hand and carefully studied them. A yellow Cat's Eye, a black shooter, and a solid red marble. The bowl was now empty. It never was empty, but it sure was now.

He recalled the question that he asked of his grandfather so many years ago.

"What if you make all bad choices and run out of marbles? What do you do then? Have you ever run out, Grandpa Brown?"

He heard his grandfather's voice in his head, "Well, no. I never have run out of marbles in the bowl. Came close a few times, but like a good goalie does, I made a few saves right at the end of the game to win and pulled it out just before the marbles ran out."

He was at a crossroads. Time to make the saves. A crossroads of his own making.

"Dad, please hand me the brown bag. It is in the top drawer of the dresser there. Be careful. Lots of marbles in there.

Mr. Brown nodded, he stood up and walked over to the dresser and grabbed the brown bag out of the drawer. He handed his son the bag and said, "I see what you mean. Almost full of marbles."

"Sure is, Dad. And now, there are three more. The bowl is officially empty."

David dropped the three marbles in the bag, pulled the draw strings tight and handed it back to his father. Mr. Brown replaced the bag in the dresser drawer.

David made a fist with his right hand and he held it in the air.

He extended his thumb in the air and said, "One. Going to stop hanging out with Jerry and those guys. Going to get back to earning straight A grades in school. Even if history is boring to me." Next, went out the pointer finger. "Two. Going to get with Coach Ray and tell him I am going to fight for that starting goalie slot back and stop missing practices and stop every puck that comes my way."

The third finger joined the rest in the air. Three fingers of decisions.

"Third, going to go over to Janie's house and tell her that I am sorry. That I love her, and share with her all the rest of my decisions, and that from now on, it is Janie and David forever. Someday, I will marry that gal. Dad, I swear that I will."

David's father put his arm around his son and pulled him in close to his body.

David Alfred Brown II said as they embraced, "Now, son, that sounds like a plan that will lead to a bowl full of marbles."

He stood up and smiled and headed for the door.

"Dinner is almost ready. Come on down. Your mother is worried about you."

"Okay, Dad. I will be down in a minute. Thanks for the pep talk. Thanks for everything."

"Of course. I love you."

"Love you too, Dad."

For many years, David remained puzzled as to why Grandpa Brown did not give his own son a bowl full of marbles of his own. David now knew why. His father was so brilliant that he did not need them.

On that following Saturday, after a date at the movies with his beloved Janie and a few moonlight kisses, David A. Brown III walked over to his dresser, opened the top drawer, and pulled out the little brown burlap bag. After tugging on the strings, David removed three marbles, and walked over to the bowl and dropped them in the bowl. Three marbles. A few days later there were six. A week later, there were ten more.

About three weeks later, on the old table, full of wear and tear and classic edges and nicks and love, on a white crocheted white doily, sat a bowl full of marbles.

It was Christmas Day in 1986 and David Alfred Brown III lifted one single marble out of the bowl. It was a red Cat's Eye. He lingered there for a bit of time, while studying the bowl full of marbles. His right hand clutched the marble, while in his left hand, he held the box with the precious engagement ring inside. Christmas Day seemed like the perfect day to propose to Janie Perkins. Just yesterday, at Christmas Eve dinner, David caught Mr. Wilford Perkins and asked for his daughter's hand in marriage. He eagerly provided his full blessings on the proposed union.

It was time. He hoped and prayed that at the end of this glorious day, when he arrived home after a grand and wonderful family celebration, and a special moment in their lives, and sharing kisses of joy and of love that the single red Cat's Eye marble would be back in the bowl.

It was.

David Wilford Brown Junior was a curious and intelligent young man. At eight years of age, he was quite advanced in his reading skills, his mathematics, and his overall school studies. The comment that his teachers always commonly noted was that "David is very intelligent and his mind wanders. As if his studies bore him because he always is looking answers and asking many questions."

The sign of high intelligence is often an inquisitive mind. With questions often come answers; with answers come more questions.

They called him "Little David."

It was Christmas Day in 2024 and the Brown family gathered to enjoy the hope, joy, love, and peace of the graceful and glorious holiday. Little David and his older sister joined in the celebration, too. After opening their presents and enjoying the grandeur and excitement of an early Christmas Day at their own home, it was the stereotypical. "Over the river and through the wood's journey to Grandpa and Grandma Brown's house they go!"

Out of the corner of Grandpa Brown's eyes, he watched

his grandson, David Wilford Brown Junior, wander away from the bright lights and beauty of the Christmas tree, from his sister, and his cousins, and from the gathering, to head upstairs. He knew that it was not to use the bathroom on the second floor. Grandpa Brown recognized that lick in his grandson's eye. It was time to go exploring and his grandfather was interested as to what the mission was that Little David had in mind.

Grandma Janie Brown smiled at her husband and Grandpa Brown smiled back in return. He then looked over to their son, David Wilford Brown, and their son smiled and nodded to both his mother and his father. He knew it was time.

They all knew.

Grandpa Brown excused himself from the circle of family and the cheer, and the stories, and he climbed up the long wooden hill to share more time, more holiday joy, and make some more memories with his grandson.

Grandpa Brown found Little David in the spare room, carefully studying the bowl full of marbles.

"Grandpa, I always wanted to ask you. I guess that I am older now and you will tell me. What are these marbles for? In this bowl. They are very cool. I love the colors. I know not to touch stuff. Unless, I ask first. You were a hockey goalie and then a hockey coach. I don't know why you would have marbles in a bowl. I would like to know. Please."

Grandpa Brown bent down and kneeled next to his grandson. In the spare room. Where he watched his hockey games and his beloved wife knitted and read books, and she pretended as she had since the day that they first met that she enjoyed hockey.

"Well, little David, let me tell you about this bowl, and

this table, and this crocheted white doily. You see, my grandfather and grandmother, they would be your great-great-grandparents, well, for Christmas one year, they gave to me, my greatest Christmas present of all time. Yes, indeed. . .."

Every day, in our lifetimes, we all face choices and decisions. Hundreds, maybe a thousand. Who knows how many?

Sometimes, we make good choices; other times, not so good choices. We are all human, and we all make mistakes. The key is to try as hard as we can every single day to make the right choices. For yourself. For your loved ones, for your neighbors, for God, and for the joy of life.

A bowl full of marbles.

THE END

2

Flash!

Mr. Ebenezer Scrooge's Resume

Objective: To obtain a part-time position promoting Christmas, and hope, joy, and love.

Attributes: Learns well from mistakes. Good with ghosts and things that go bump in the night. Superior money counting skills. Loves and honors Christmas and the holiday season.

Education: Graduated with honors from a remote boarding school when Senior Scrooge (father) shipped me off there in exile.

Experience: Apprenticed in money lending and trades and such from working with Old Fezziwig. Taught the value of money, taught nuances of business and respecting others, taught about hard work, Christmas parties, drinking porter, dancing, being jovial and happy. How to be glorious. Fell in love.

Career: Forgot how to be glorious. No longer danced. No longer jovial. Worshipped money and power. Ditched love. Forgot every lesson learned from Old Fezziwig.

Met Jacob Marley. Went into business with Mr. Marley. Opened money lending and trading firm.

Co-Owner-Partner: Scrooge and Marley for over 40 years.

Connived, cheated, became evil and very rich.

Dined in melancholy taverns.

Marley died, and I inherited the company and everything associated with it.

Became an evil-money-grubbing miser. Continued legacy of cheating, conniving, and being grumpy and evil. Treated everyone, including my employee(s) very poorly and was very happy to do so.

Despised Christmas and laughter and my only living family member.

Counted money for fun.

Jacob Marley was my only friend and after he died, I had no other friends and only spoke of business and how to make money and cheat, connive, and become wealthier and wealthier.

Had an amazing encounter with four ghosts (Yes. Technically, there were four ghosts. Despite rumors, and non-factual testimonies of only three ghosts) on the Christmas Eve anniversary of my old partner's death. In fact, Jacob Marley returned to visit me as the "Head Ghost." Not sure if it was undigested beef, or some moldy cheese, or a dab of mustard, or an underdone potato, but there were ghosts.

I am quite sure of it; and you will not get me to change my mind or my testimony.

Changed my ways.

Realized the importance of family.

Became very, very happy.

Remembered how to dance and how to love.

Tiny Tim lived because I paid for the best doctors and the best medical care for him.

Realized life is very, very short; make the most of it.

Dined in happy pubs.

Loved everything about Christmas and life.

Became glorious again.

Summary: Give me a chance. I will teach you about Christmas, and love, joy, and hope. Will teach you how to love life and be glorious. Will work for no charge. I do not need the money.

And be happy to do so.

God bless us. Everyone.

Spark

Lonely

"If everyone lies awake in bed in the middle of the night and they hear The Lonely Train Whistle; then why is the whistle still lonely?"

3

Flash!

Charlie's Bar and Grille

It was a bitterly cold day, and the wind blew hard and with a purpose; the kind of cold that worked its way through your clothes and into a person's soul.

It was New Year's Eve. Yet right here, and right now, there was no celebration.

The giant steel monster huffed and puffed and swung its bucket with fury at the structure. The first blow inflicted heavy damage. The side wall began to crumble down to the ground below it. Steel, and glass, and concrete, and sections of the roof flew in all directions. It was a deathblow.

On the front wall of Charlie's Bar and Grille.

The sign out on the main street still proclaimed that it was Charlie's Bar and Grille. Even while the steel monster inflicted the deathblows on the building.

The walls and the roof and the windows all came crumbling down and fell in great piles of dust mixed with sadness and memories.

He stood on the outside of the metal construction fence, looking in at the scene, with his overcoat on, his gloves on his hands, and his wool hat on his head. Even with his winter clothing, he buried his hands in his pockets to capture warmth.

"You can watch, but please stay well outside the construction fence! Safety first!"

The foreman on the construction site yelled over to the man standing outside the fence, watching the demolition.

The man waved back and cupped his hands around his mouth to project his words against the wind and answered.

"I will!" And he watched the deathblows and fought back some tears. So many good times there; meeting so many people. Happy, sad, angry, and otherwise. The hockey games on the overhead televisions, the baseball games, and the cooking shows. Yes! One of the bartenders loved to cook and always had a cooking show playing on her shift.

"Hey, Paulie! I see you could not stay away, either. Huh?"

The man turned around and saw that it was Mary! The long-time late shift bartender. She was making her way over to where he stood. Mary still looked about the same; a little older, a little more bent. As the man was older and a little bent now, too.

"My goodness! Mary! So wonderful to see you! Of course, I had to come and watch. I saw them build the place all those years ago and now, well, I am watching them tear it all down."

They shared some hugs and some more welcoming conversation. Then they turned their attention back to the scene as more walls came crumbling down.

"It is so sad, Mary. So, so, sad."

"Sure is, Paulie. Sure is. You still working in the office building next door to here?"

"I am. Twenty-six years now. Counting down my days, now. What are you doing now?"

"I tend bar downtown on the weekends, but mostly work as a nanny for some wealthy folks. It is okay, but not the same as Charlie's. Remember the good-time nachos with cheese? You always ordered those at happy hour. When you came over with your work buddies."

"Sure do. And you would deliver them and say the same thing every time."

Paulie looked at Mary to see if she recalled her words.

Mary smiled and said, "I put extra good times in there for you, Paulie!"

They hugged and laughed.

Then the front wall of the restaurant collapsed under the force of a deathblow and when it did so, it revealed the bar. Where they shared those good times.

"Look there, Mary. My stool. Right next to the drink pickup hole."

"Sure is. Yup. There is where I worked for close to twenty years. My first job. I was the first employee hired. The longest tenure, too. It is heartbreaking. The recession closed so many businesses around here," Mary said, as she waved at the surroundings, "you were one of the longest customers. Maybe the longest. You survived the recession and returned. Then the pandemic was the end of it. No one wanted to work anymore. The managers could only cover so many shifts. The end. I remember when happy hour was six deep at that bar."

"So do I."

A voice from behind them. It was Heather! The other long-term bartender. Still as pretty as she ever was! More hugs, more tears! More sharing of memories. Then Chris arrived! And Lisa. And Julian! Dear Julian! And Bastion the front-end manager! It was a glorious reunion. Full of memories, and tears, and now, the bitter wind was not as bitter as the group huddled around for protection.

Paulie shared a profound and humorous memory. Although, at the time, it seemed more frightening than humorous.

"Hey guys! Remember that terribly hot and humid late afternoon, when the sky turned black and purple and all our phones and the TVs and radios started sounding the tornado alerts?"

Heather joined in first, as the group recalled the memory.

"Sure do! We are were scared stiff! Bastion rounded us all up and stuffed us in the beer keg cooler in the middle of the kitchen! We sure got to know each well stuffed in there like sardines."

Heather finished speaking. She turned to Paulie and winked at him.

"Yup. Safest place. In fact, there it is. Not much left of it, now." Bastion explained as he turned and pointed to the wreckage in front of them.

Chris piped up and shared a touching memory.

"Remember when those two older folks got engaged in their favorite booth? They came in every Saturday afternoon for years! Then they got married in front of their favorite booth. The booth by the back window! What were their names?"

Mary knew.

"Laurie and Howard. Got married right there."

Mary pointed, but there was not too much left to identify within the mass of wreckage.

The giant monster had eaten its way to about the middle of the facility—there was the kitchen. Stoves and cookers, and metal exhaust fan hoods, and wires and pipes, and more dust scooped up and bashed and thrown and destroyed into piles of dust and spent memories.

Suddenly, the bitter cold took over their space. Sadness returned like a heavy fog and enveloped the small group of friends. Tears flowed once again.

The giant monster was still hungry to devour the building.

Chris was first to leave and then the others slowly bid farewell as the cold infiltrated their bodies and souls. They all exchanged new year's wishes, their phone numbers, and contacts; although, as it usually is in these situations, they knew they would most likely never speak or meet again.

When Mary finally left, Paulie stood alone, as he first did.

Alone for a few more minutes while he ran more memories through his mind. Then it was time to say good bye. He wiped a tear from his eye, turned on his heels and slowly made his way back to where he parked his car at the building where he worked for all these years.

He left the sign out on the main street that still proclaimed that it was Charlie's Bar and Grille. Paulie left his memories. He left parts and pieces of his soul that the wind had left untouched, and he left it all there in the piles of dust and debris.

It was a bitter cold day, and the wind blew hard and with a purpose; the kind of cold that worked its way past your clothes and into a person's soul.

It was New Year's Eve; yet here there was no celebration. Only some memories and dust.

4

Flash!

The Miracle of the Lights

The daughter gave it her all to take care of her family. Her heart, her love, and her soul. A commitment of profound depth and inner strength all layered with intense compassion.

She felt as if she owed them all. They gave her life and her joy.

Her parents, her grandmother—all very close to her soul. Her grandfather passed years earlier, but they all fondly remembered him, too.

They were all loving, religious, and compassionate. It was a very special family.

Her fondest times in her life she spent with them and her own family. In, a time that now seemed as if it were ages ago. Or even longer.

Yet, Father Time remains undefeated.

First, the grandmother grew old and feeble and the family rallied around her and loved her and supported her through the battles with health and old age. Weak eyesight and a weak heart, and some severe mobility issues. Her deep religious beliefs sustained her and her family. The grandmother knew God's plan and love.

Christmastime was always special to the family. They celebrated the religious aspect of the holiday as well as the secular aspect. The daughter and her husband and their small children made it all very special. No one could recall whose idea it actually was; but it might have been the daughter's husband.

He held Christmas in a special place in his heart.

When Grammy, as they lovingly called her, became bedridden, the daughter's husband suggested that the family decorate her bedroom with Christmas joy. A small Christmas tree, holly with small lights, and in a special touch, plastic candelabras with battery-operated lights that mimicked candle flames, and that hung over the door to the bedroom. They all glowed in Christmas celebration, and even with feeble eyesight, Grammy could see and enjoy the colors and the brilliance of the broadcasting of Christmas. Particularly, the candle candelabras and their lights hanging over the door. For some reason, Grammy focused on them. Perhaps it was her eyesight, perhaps it was some other reason, but those lights on the door provided great joy.

Such a simple and pleasurable little thing, that we take for granted at holiday celebrations for so many years, but when the light of life fades and flickers, we focus on the things that we never should take for granted. Even after the Christmas holidays passed, the family left the lights up and turned on, and the enjoyment they brought was immeasurable. Grammy did not have a calendar. She did not realize the date, and that Christmas passed. The lights provided simple joy.

Sadly, Grammy passed on to her heavenly rewards. Gone; never forgotten.

When her parents became old and feeble, the daughter took charge. With her husband's blessing and support, she moved into their home, now located in another state, and the daughter worked day and night to tend to their needs; to their health; to their lives, in order to make them as comfortable as she could do so.

And the tradition of the Christmas lights continued. Especially the plastic candelabras on the doors. . ..

Sadly, after a long illness and a period of feebleness, the daughter's father passed on to his heavenly rewards.

Gone; never forgotten.

When her blessed mother became bedridden, the Christmas lights reappeared. At one point, the candelabras failed, and the bulbs were difficult to find. The daughter's husband found replacement's and sent them to his wife. Her mother loved them; staring at the comforting glow. It provided such simple joy. The date did not matter, nor did the fact that Christmas was long since in the past. The lights glowed year-round. The daughter never turned them off. The lights of the plastic candelabras glowed on. Through the pain, through the suffering; a light.

A simple beacon of hope. Jesus Christ.

* "As long as I am in the world, I am the light of the world."

Sadly, after a long illness and a period of feebleness, the daughter's mother passed on to her heavenly rewards.

Gone; never forgotten.

The daughter's tears fell like rain. Her heart ached. She had given it her all. Her best. Heaven smiled down at her saintly efforts. Love drives love and love conquers all. Love weathers the greatest storms. Love lights the darkest nights.

A beacon of hope.

The daughter returned home. To her life. To her family, but she never forgot her love, the joy, the simple things, such as the lights.

The Christmas after her mother's passing was particularly harsh. She did not feel much like celebrating the holidays, yet out of a dusty, old box, she pulled the plastic candelabras. She hung them on a door in the main hallway of her home and lit the lights up. Remarkably, they all lit. The same batteries for years now. Never changed. The family marveled at them and decided to leave them lit. And light they did. For days and for nights, through the holidays and afterwards, the lights continued onward. Some days, they seemed dimmer. Some days, they burned brighter. A secular joy with a heavenly touch.

An ebb and flow, yet they lit.

It seemed like a miracle!

One day, her son observed the lights, and he commented as he touched each one of them.

"For Grammy. For Popo. For Ma. It seems spooky that they still light. After all these years on those same batteries. They still light."

The daughter smiled and shook her head.

After a period of solace, the daughter said, "It is not spooky. Batteries do not light those candelabras. Love lights them."

Never take the light for granted; not in the wind, nor the cold, nor in the harshest of times. For when the world is harsh and cruel, and illness and pain and sadness all plague us, that is when the miracle of the lights burns brightest.

* "As long as I am in the world, I am the light of the world."

* The Gospel of John Chapter 9, verse 5. The Holy Bible, King James Version. Cambridge Edition: 1769. Public Domain.

5

Flash!

Corporate Confusion

Mr. Dwayne DeMercotroit was the big boss. His title was Executive Director of, well, something or other. Yet, no one actually knew what his title was, or exactly what he did at the Whiz-Bang Corporation.

Dwayne was tall, and very thin, and he had eyebrows like two leaping caterpillars. He wore his hair short, yet his hair stood on end. His face looked as if he was perpetually walking into an eighty-miles-per-hour windstorm. Squinty eyes and a pushed-in face.

Dwayne had a fancy corner office on the ninth floor of the corporate headquarters. The tenth floor housed the super-demi-god executive suite. Dwayne was one level below the demi-gods, but his goal was to land on the tenth floor someday.

His administrative assistant sat outside of Dwayne's office, but the telephone on her desk never rang. She never worked on her computer. The monitor was off. She did not have any pens, or pencils, or papers on her desk. There was not even a file cabinet in her cubicle. Mostly, she simply sat there and waited for something to happen. And checked her lipstick.

Mr. DeMercotroit always wore a suit and necktie that was too short, and a plaid jacket, with black shoes that squeaked when he walked up and down the hallways of the massive corporate headquarters. And Dwayne always walked around, squinting, and staring at fellow employees, while carrying a coffee cup in one hand and a manila folder in the other hand.

Dwayne mentioned that he served in the military. But he never said what branch, or when, or what he did, or where. He told everyone that he graduated with a master's degree in something, from Blabbo University, but no one ever heard of that institute of higher learning. His undergraduate degree came from Philanderer College in Maple Syrupville, Vermont. No one ever heard of that college or location, either. Dwayne also played professional baseball; had a tryout with a professional basketball team, but had to quit because of a twisted ankle. He swam the English Channel twice and scaled Pike's Peak once.

Only once.

Dwayne said he was going to scale it twice, but it was easier than he thought, so he never gave it a second try.

Because it was too costly and confusing, the Human Resources Department at the Whiz-Bag Corporation did very limited background checks on their hires. . ..

Frankie Fankenhauser worked in the mailroom at the corporate headquarters. A summer temp job. He just graduated high school. Until he started college in the fall of this year, this was a outstanding summer job for him. Frankie was going to be a business major, so this little jaunt in a major corporation would provide some valuable insight into the corporate world. He needed to save up money for a car for college.

Frankie stood in front of the desk of Mr. DeMercotroit's administrative assistant.

She looked up at him and smiled.

"How can I help you?"

"Hello. I am Frankie Frankenhauser. I have an appointment with Mr. DeMercotroit for ten this morning."

She shrugged her shoulders, looked at her watch and said, "That's a lot of Franks. I know nothing about it. But it is one minute to ten. You are very prompt. Go right in."

Frankie nervously knocked on the open door of the office of the big super-chief. He was not sure what he did wrong! Maybe he miss-delivered some important mail?

Mr. DeMercotroit bellowed from behind his desk, and he stood up and waved.

His caterpillar eyebrows flapped like windshield wipers in a thunderstorm as he spoke.

"Come right in! Sit down here in the guest chair, Frankfurter! Sit down. Notice my plush carpet, the fantastic elegant furnishings, and the fancy executive office I have here!"

Frankie crept slowly into the office, as he looked all around.

As he carefully sunk into the guest chair, and the big boss sat in his high-back executive chair, Frankie sputtered out some words.

"It is very nice. Beautiful office, sir. However, my name is Frankie Frankenhauser. Not Frankfurter."

Mr. DeMercotroit waved dismissively and said, "Oh well, whatever. That's a lot of Franks."

"Have I done something wrong, sir?"

"Frankly . . . get it?"

"Yes, I get it, sir."

"Frankly, yes! I have been putting it off for weeks and weeks to meet with you," Mr. DeMercotroit said, as he then placed his hands on top of a pile of at least one-hundred manila folders, "I have your file in here somewhere. I have to file all of these, but never take care of it, but I have noticed how you procrastinate terribly in your job duties and are not efficient at all!"

Frankie screwed his face up and stared at the big boss.

"I do? I mean, I sort and deliver mail. My supervisor never complains about my work. I am a temp in the mailroom for the summer."

"Exactly! All I ever see you do is walk around here with mail and packages in your hands and deliver them to offices, while you roll a mail cart up and down the hallways!"

"Ah, yes, that is my job, sir."

Mr. DeMercotroit screwed his face up like a corkscrew and asked, "It is?"

"Yes, sir."

Mr. DeMercotroit pounded his desk with his fist and stood up.

"Well, now. That settles that. Keep up the good work! Come on over here, Frankenfurter. Let me show you this photograph of Pikes Peak. I scaled that sucker with my bare hands while wearing some baseball spikes, and was going to climb it again, but. . .."

Later that day, on his lunch break, Frankie called his father.

"Dad, I have been thinking. I changed my mind. Instead of college, I want to go to trade school. Plumbing. Work with you. Take over Frankenhauser Plumbing and Heating, someday when you retire. The family business. I am thinking that this corporate business world might not be for me."

Spark

Blue Skies

"We can't always have blue skies; otherwise, we would not have rain, and snow, and fog, and dark and stormy clouds. We need them all. Simply remember that underneath all the dark and stormy skies; therein are the blue skies."

Spark

Full Moons and Such

"Why is it that during a full moon, it is everyone *else* who is acting weird and strange?"

6

Short

Your Move

He was fourteen years old. Tall, handsome, athletic, and he had long, floppy blonde hair with red highlights. He was intelligent and curious, too. Usually, he wore canvas sneakers and tee shirts with his favorite rock and roll music bands' logos emblazoned on them. He was not fashionable or in vogue or popular in high school; however, he did not care about any of that. Even at fourteen years of age, he lived his life on his terms.

It was an old New Jersey city and the main street overflowed with traffic flowing in and out from downtown to the boroughs beyond. Trucks and buses and cars and people. A main thoroughfare. Old homes lined the main street; typical city homes, small lots with small backyards. Hot and steamy in the summer and frigid in the winter. There was no such thing as air-conditioning here and most of the boilers were questionable.

This old neighborhood, on the outskirts of the city, remained ethnically diverse. English, Irish, Welsh, Scottish, Germans, Italians, Jewish, Spanish, Black, and Russians and Polish and folks of all sorts of walks of life and from many countries.

The young man loved the diversity. His curiosity was always on alert. He always wanted to learn of new foods, holidays, new customs, new languages, new styles. And some very old ones, too. And he loved learning about an watching the celebrations of the different holidays that the diverse neighborhood celebrated. He was a holiday sort of guy.

Right now, he had his eye set on a very pretty, fourteen-year-old Dominican gal . . ..

This one particular old home sat next to the dye factory on the main street. It was four stories high; one old store on the bottom level and three apartments above. Each apartment was small. No larger than eight hundred square feet at the most. The store was a carpet store. Repairs and weaving. Specialty carpets.

The young man's grandfather told him that the building and store were full of new occupants. Circassians. A race of people hailing from the Caucasus Mountain regions. They once had their own country; Circassia, but Russia conquered them and the people fled to many parts of the world. Many were religious and political refugees. Now, this small group lived in the old city, too. The new residents added to the diversity of the old neighborhood.

The young man walked past the store and apartment building every day on the way to high school and back to his home. He grew up here. Only a few blocks south of where the home stood. He had seen the building and store change in use and appearance many times over the years. Now, it was a new wave of residents. The carpets in the windows of the store fascinated him. The colors and the craftsmanship. The weaving and patterns of the cloth were magnificent. He studied them; for his vocational goals remained with working with his hands. His high school was a trade school and working with electricity was his ambition.

The two Circassian men were very old. It was late spring and not warm, but not cold either. Despite the weather, each of them wore a heavy wool hat on his head. So did his partner on the other side of the table. They both wore black robes over black pants and black shirts under the robes. Around their necks were tightly wrapped leather necklaces of about mid-chest length with a stone on the end of them. On their feet were tall brown boots; made of leather and the laces of the boots, worked their way upward on a steady climb. The men sat on small chairs on opposite sides of a small table that contained a chessboard with wooden chess pieces. The table was set on the sidewalk out front of the carpet store and old apartment building. On the table there also was a small dish with some cornbread inside and an elegant white porcelain teapot with gorgeous blue patterns inscribed on it. Each man had teacups next to their playing position. They both leaned over the chessboard and studied the game. A few pieces sat next to each of the teacups. The match was only a few moves old.

The young man made his way home from school. The two old men playing the chess match on the sidewalk fascinated him. Their hats, their clothing, the tea, the game. He stopped and stood next to the table and studied the game. He knew a little of the playing of the game, but not enough to play very well. The two men did not look up at the young man. They continued studying and playing, and one of the men—perhaps the oldest of the two, a man with a very long beard, a worn face, gnarly hands and fingers, and deep brown eyes—managed an advantage.

The beautiful young woman, just a teenager on the cusp of womanhood, stepped out of the side door of the building and walked over while carrying a teapot with oven mitts on her hands. She was about the same age as the young man was. Maybe a little older, but not by much. She had long brown hair, a round face, a short nose, and she wore a long white dress that swirled in many layers from short layers at her neck, to medium layers at her waist. The dress then swirled and wound its way to her ankles. Over the top of the dress, she wore a blue sweater. Her eyes met the young man's eyes, and she smiled. He smiled back.

He thought she was exotic; captivating and beautiful. She thought he was incredibly handsome.

Without much more than the smile and a nod his way, she switched the teapots and returned to the side door.

Just a moment in time. Or was it?

The men poured the fresh tea into their cups as the match drew closer to the end. The young man stood in silence while watching. Suddenly, the side door of the building opened and the young woman reappeared. She carried a teacup and set it on the table. She picked up the teapot and poured some tea into the cup, and with a smile, she handed it to the spectator.

"Tea?"

She asked and with only one word, he heard her heavy accent. Yet, he knew her English was good. Now he confirmed that she was beautiful.

Stunning.

He said, "Yes. Thank you."

He loved tea. His mum was English, and he grew up on tea.

Without another word, the young woman disappeared back into the home.

The young man knew enough of the game to gasp a little when the older man made his final move to checkmate. The two men both looked up and smiled at the young man.

The winner reached down and handed the young man the dish of cornbread and said, "Eat."

His accent was strong.

"Thank you." The young man said while he took a piece of cornbread. He smiled and sipped the tea. The oldest man asked as he pointed at the chair opposite him.

"You play?"

"I do, but I am not very good."

The other man rose and smiled, and he too pointed at the chair. They seemed to understand him. A little.

"Your move," the older man said, as his eyes flickered with delight.

Some things in life have no barriers.

It only took less than ten minutes for the young man to lose. They laughed. They smiled. The game and the joy had no language barrier. The young man shook their hands and off he went. He was late for dinner.

From behind a worn curtain on the second-floor window, the young woman watched as the young man sprinted off to home. She smiled.

The next day, the young man stopped and played again.

"Your move," the old man said.

From thereon, the young man always went first.

And then the following week, a few more matches. Months went by. Even in the hot summer months, the young man would wander up to play a few matches of chess. He had never won a single one. But he did learn that the hat was a "Papakha" and that the family fled their homeland because they were Christians. Most of the Circassians were Muslims. It seemed as if they did not fit in.

And he learned that their coats were "Chokas" and they made the hat out of sheepskin. And the young gal would come out and watch them play and interpret the languages and teach him about the Circassian ways. He learned that the young gal was engaging and beautiful and she spoke good English. He would teach her of the New Jersey and

English ways. He told her of his family and she told him of his. He learned that her name was Nadia, and he told her that his name was Paul.

With her accent, his name came out more like, "Pawel."

And suddenly, the young man no longer had eyes for a certain Dominican gal. …

She attended a religious school, but mostly, she learned her studies at home. The oldest man was her grandfather and the other man was her uncle. They repaired and cleaned and made the carpets in the first-floor store. She lived in the second-floor apartment, along with her grandmother, and aunts and uncles and a few cousins who all lived on the other floors. They all lived in the one building. A crowded place! Her parents were still in Asia, waiting for asylum to escape the persecution.

After the chess match, the two teenagers would sit and talk and watch the city life go by.

And fall in love.

Then one day, in that following October, on a crisp fall day; it happened! The young man finally won a chess match! They all celebrated! They all danced for joy; together, on that old city sidewalk. In front of the small table.

The grandmother brought out a bottle of wine in one of the most wonderful glass vases that anyone ever saw. It was blue, with yellow streaks and some dashes of red. The young woman explained that since they were Christian, they did drink wine for Communion at church and at special celebrations. And this was one. The young man told them all that he was a Christian, too. A Lutheran.

Everyone received a small pour of wine in special glasses. . ..

Ages and drinking laws did not apply. It was their

culture.

The next time they sat down for a chess match, the grandfather smiled, patted his chest, and said, "My move."

Fourteen, led to fifteen, and then sixteen, and the matches became more infrequent. The grandfather was very old, and he was very ill. It made everyone very sad.

Father Time; still undefeated.

If the weather was fine, then on most of those days, on his way home from school, the young man stopped and chatted with the young gal and they sat and watched the traffic and the world go by.

At times, it seemed as there was no one else in their world. Only them.

And he did not have the courage to kiss her or ask her for a date.

One day, in September, he saw her sitting on the stoop of the storefront and he knew. Her tears told the story. His chess partner was gone.

Paul went to the funeral in a tie that was too short, shoes that were too tight, and a suit that did not fit. He did not understand a single word of the language of the church service, but he knew when to pray.

Some things in life have no barriers.

Nadia thought he was the most handsome young man that she ever saw.

The following week, he walked by and Nadia was waiting on the stoop for him to come along. She wore a white dress; with those same glorious layers and a beautiful wrap of the deepest blue in a silken weave on her head. In her hand, she held a small box. Nadia jumped up when he came along. Her heart always jumped at the sight of him.

She smiled a sparkling smile that could melt ice.

"Here, Pawel. Grandpa-pa wanted you to have this. Sit. Open. Please." She handed off the box and excitedly returned to the cement stoop and patted the concrete for him to sit next to him. He did so and opened the box and pulled out the chessboard and the wooden chess pieces. All carefully wrapped and preserved.

Paul's eyes teared up, and so did Nadia's eyes.

"Oh, Nadia. I can't take this. . .."

She gently placed her hands over his as they rested on the top of the box.

"Oh yes, you can. Must. Pawel. You must."

And they studied each other's eyes. And he so wanted to kiss her and ask her to go for ice cream up the road at the Haledon Diner.

She studied his eyes and pleaded with them for him to kiss her. She smiled as she still tightly held his hands over the top of the box.

"Your move," she said in a gentle whisper. Her words came out of her mouth as if they danced on sunbeams.

They kissed. It was long, and it was glorious. He thought how she tasted like the sweetest candy that he had ever tasted. Her lips were soft, and he felt as if he absorbed within her soul as they kissed.

She felt as if her all of her dreams just came true.

Behind the curtain on the second floor of the building, a feeble old grandmother peered in at the scene and she smiled. Her tears fell like rain. But they were joyful and nourishing tears. They were tears for the hope of the future and for the hope that a new life in a new land brings.

"Do you wanna go for ice cream?" Paul finally mustered up the courage to ask Nadia as they broke their kiss.

"Of course. I must have chocolate."

"Vanilla."

Some things in life have no barriers.

7

Flash!

Lungs Like a Blowtorch

Ah, yes, the nostalgia. It tends to stay with you in a very special way. Longing for the way that things used to be in such simpler times.

"Timmmmmyyy! Ariannnnna!"

The call beckoned throughout the neighborhood. Through an open upstairs window. Hands cupped around her mouth. Mother Esposito took another deep breath and once again launched into the call.

"Time for dinnnnnnerrrrr!"

Mother Esposito was rather large, and she had lungs like a blowtorch.

There were no cellphones. No internet. No texting. There were simpler and better ways of communicating.

Old city neighborhoods are very special and so unique. The nuances that they have are more than intriguing. They captivate.

This old city neighborhood had it all. From Goldberg's Jewish Delicatessen on the corner of North 12th Street and Belmont Avenue, serving up that golden mustard on top of the hot pastrami, to the German Pork Store, to the Campus Sweet Shop, to Gabby's Cabin, it was all diverse and special and unique. Unless you grew up there; it was very difficult to describe to a person that did not experience it. And the nuances of growing up there stick in your mind forever.

It was only three weeks after Christmas. January. The longest month with approximately three-hundred-and eighty-four days. Or thereabouts.

It was a bitter cold Wednesday, and overnight, there had been about six inches or thereabouts of snow. Unlike these days; no media-induced panic occurred. No one hid under their kitchen table in fear over a few inches of snow.

Work continued. School was open; just a normal day. The stores were all open, including the supermarkets and the shelves, all stocked with the normal numbers of products and goods. The mailman and the milkman all delivered their goods and made the rounds. The city buses all ran. The world revolved normally.

The city snowplows came barging through and made the streets slightly cavernous; but that was part of the silent, snowy magic.

He lived in the small house right next door to the Esposito's house. He was a devoted husband and father to two children. Off he went to work at his same time. When hearing of the forecast, he set his alarm for an hour and a half early. He needed to get up early to allow for the snow. His shift at the machine shop started at six in the morning. That three-thirty alarm was hell, but up he was. Hat, overcoat, gloves, scarf, and boots. Snow shovel in hand; shovel the driveway and front sidewalk while he warmed up the old car, load some bags of sand in the trunk for weight, chains on the wheels, and off to work he went. No allowance for calling out of work! No excuses. This was the day and age of commitment; not the time to be a cupcake.

Off the kiddies went to school, like teetering penguins making their stiff way along the snowy terrain. Sledding, and snowball fights, and snowmen, and fun!

By three in the afternoon, the snowstorm was almost a memory. Only the lingering snow piles on the edges of life and the roads and sidewalks remained as a testimony to its passing through. The kiddies went in reverse and trudged home. There was homework to do but there was also sledding, and snowball fights, and snowmen and fun! The father made his way back home after the shift ended, along what were now mostly clear streets. Just some patches of ice and snow here and there.

The Esposito's house was small. Narrow, but two stories tall with a basement below. A wooden porch with stone steps. The bedrooms were on the upper floor. Kitchen, dining room, living room on the first floor. One bathroom upstairs. The home sat in a most unusual location. Next to an old restaurant; they shared a common driveway. Just off a city side street. If the home was a thousand square feet, that was an exaggeration. The Esposito family were a New Jersey-Italian family. Catholic and proud to be so. They went to mass most every morning at Saint Gerard's parish. The children attended Saint Gerard's Parochial School. Father, mother, grandfather, grandmother, and two children. All in one-thousand square feet of city living. When Grandma (Nonna) Esposito slow-simmered her gravy on Sundays and Wednesdays for her pasta dishes, you could smell the heavenly aroma for two city blocks. A luxury was a color television in the living room. They always gathered around the set and watched Lawrence Welk on Saturday evenings.

This snowy evening was Wednesday, and it was the traditional spaghetti dinner night. You could not smell Nonna Esposito's gravy slow-simmering throughout the neighborhood on this snowy evening. They kept the windows closed tightly and the glorious aromas could not escape.

The father pulled into the driveway and shut off the

engine. He grabbed his lunch pail and headed for the back door.

The father burst in through the back door of the home and it was cozy and warm and it was inviting. It was now four-thirty in the afternoon. He had left the home around twelve hours earlier. A long day. To say the least.

Yet, he felt wonderful. The kitchen table was set, his beer mug had a cold beer poured in it; his newspaper sat next to his place. An old table radio on a shelf played some easy listening music from a local radio station. His wife kissed his cheek and waved to his seat at the head of the table. She had done her hair up and had some gentle perfume on. The mother of this family was very lovely.

"Sit down, honey. Relax now. Have your beer. How was your day? You must be starving!"

"I am, baby. Ah, ya know. The bosses are on our asses. After the Christmas shutdown. We gotta make those numbers! Production. What's for dinner? Smells great!"

"I defrosted the leftover turkey from Christmas and New Year's Day. Turkey soup, some white meat, some dark meat. Stuffing, green beans, and salad and your beer. I even got your pickled onions."

Nothing went to waste in those days.

"Ya the best."

The father took a sip of beer and he grabbed his newspaper and started to read it. Had to check the hockey scores from last night.

"Where are the kids? They ain't gonna be late for dinner. Are they?"

The mother smiled. She knew. It was Wednesday.

"Oh no. They came home and did their homework and then went to the vacant lot with their sleds to sled down the plowed snow piles."

The father looked precariously over the edge of his newspaper at his wife, as his wife added, "They went with the Esposito kids."

He nodded and went back to his beer and the hockey scores.

From behind the newspaper, the father said, "Okay. Mother Esposito will call them all home any minute now. That woman has lungs like a blowtorch."

Almost on queue; above the easy listening music, the call went out from the Esposito's house.

"Timmmmmyyy! Adriannnnna!"

The call beckoned throughout the neighborhood. Through an open upstairs window. Hands cupped around her mouth. Mother Esposito took another deep breath and once again launched into the call.

"Time for dinnnnnnerrrrr!"

Mother Esposito was rather large, and, indeed, she had lungs like a blowtorch.

A few minutes later, their children burst through the door—red-faced and cold, but that turkey soup and dinner would do the trick.

Old city neighborhoods are very special and so unique. The nuances that they have are more than intriguing. They captivate.

They tend to stay with you forever.

Spark

Today Versus Tomorrow

"If today seems overwhelming, then just wait for tomorrow. If tomorrow is overwhelming, too, then just settle for today."

Spark

Young Lovers and Old Lovers

"I am not sure why movies, and television, and the media only ever depict young lovers. They ought to depict old lovers. They have more experience in the hurt, the pain, the passion, and the ebbs and flow of love than young lovers do. It would be a helluva lot more realistic."

8

Flash!

A White Pearl Necklace
A Bright Orange Corduroy Dress

She saw him standing there. Next to his locker in the west hallway of their high school. He was the new guy in the high school; tall, lean, a wave of blonde hair that swept to the side, wonderful cheekbones and a smile that melted every female's heart.

He was lean but full of muscles. He was going to be the starting quarterback this fall for the football team.

The word was that his father accepted a transfer for a new job and here he was. . ..

She felt as if she was a rather "Plain Jane" sort of gal. Nothing special. Kinda tall for sixteen years of age. Straight brown hair, kind'a of a nothing figure, with no hips, no butt, small breasts. No pouty lips, no endearing eyes, with lipid pools of bliss flowing within them. No high cheekbones.

Nothing special. In her eyes. Yet, she loved to have fun.

She gazed at him and thought he was the most handsome man in the world.

She wore a white pearl necklace around her neck and a bright orange corduroy dress. Not exactly the fashionable pick for the day in 1977.

They were her grandmother's pearls.

He wore black dungarees and a black tee shirt with

some type of football team logo emblazoned upon it. The latest and greatest in fashionable sneakers on his feet.

She did not know of modern football teams. Nothing.

All the most popular gals flocked around him. The head cheerleader for the football team. The co-head-cheerleader. The stunningly beautiful gal who was the leader of the anti-establishment team of gals. Girls who protested the war and the government, and smoked the good weed in the woods behind the school and drank cheap ripple wine smuggled from the leader of the anti-establishment group of boys. These gals wore their jeans low upon their hips; they wore wide belts with peace-sign belt buckles, and they wore tight shirts with no brassieres.

They all adored him from the first glance. They were all amongst the smartest. The most beautiful. The most popular.

She did not stand a chance. Yet, while they were adoring him and flocking to him, he lifted an eye to her. Just an eye. A simple glance.

He smiled.

She smiled back and then she shyly toyed with the floor with her shoe.

Late in the day, on a Thursday, just before the big weekend game, when the masses had left him, he caught her when she was spinning the combination to her hallway locker. He caught her by surprise. To say the least.

"Say, I would like to ask you out on a date. I would like to ask if you would like to stop off at the sandwich shop on the way home from school and play some pinball. Listen to music on the jukebox. Get a sandwich and have a soda? My treat."

Her heart leaped in her throat. Once she regained control, she smiled, and her voice came out of mouth as if it was the squeaks of a mouse.

"Sure. I . . . mean, yes!"

Her enthusiasm was slightly embarrassing.

"What is your name?" He asked, as his long eyelashes licked his brows. "I am Steve."

He extended his hand and waited for her response.

Her palms were sweaty, and she knew it, but here was no time to wipe them dry. They shook hands.

"Margaret. I mean, most people call me, Peggy."

"I will call you, Margaret. Always."

"Okay. . .."

Their first date. And they came very close to sharing a first kiss. Maybe they did. And maybe they didn't. But they sure kissed on the second date.

From that moment onward . . . they laughed. They rejoiced. They had spirit in their hearts and they had fun. Never was their such joy!

His smile melted her heart. He was the most handsome man she had ever seen.

Ten years later, shortly after the birth of their first child, they lay in their bed after putting the baby to sleep, and she finally had the courage to ask him the question that she begged to ask him for these past ten years.

"Why did you ever ask me out on that first date? You had your pick of some many others? So many beautiful women. . .."

He leaned over, and gently kissed her cheek, and then her lips, and lovingly played with her brown hair and gently tucked it behind her ears.

His answer arrived.

"Margaret. Because, the first time that I saw you and our eyes met, you smiled. You spoke to my heart and my soul. You wore white pearls in a glorious necklace around your neck, and on your heavenly body, you wore a bright orange corduroy dress that shouted at me . . . I am so different and I am so special! Then you toyed with the floor with your shoe to tell me that you were interested but shy. Yet, I could tell, no, I knew, that any woman who dressed like that loved to have fun. From your head to your toe. I longed for a person to share fun with. Forever! Yes! I fell in love with you right there and right then. And forever. And I must tell you." He leaned in and kissed her deeply before speaking again, "There are no women or any woman, more beautiful than you are. Margaret."

He smiled at her.

She smiled back.

She gazed at him and thought he was the most beautiful man in the world.

A bright orange corduroy dress.

They were her grandmother's pearls.

And they had fun.

Forever.

Spark

Put Forth

“When it is put forth what humankind can create to glorify God’s great creation, you realize that the creation and the glory of God are both limitless and unimaginable all at the same time.”

"He hath made every thing beautiful in his time."

* Ecclesiastes Chapter 3, verse 11. The Holy Bible, King James Version. Cambridge Edition: 1769. Public Domain.

9

Flash!

Lonely Classic Movies

Glenn Willingham wore a crew cut, he always wore old-fashioned striped neckties that were too short and pants just above his shoes. He wore clothes that always seemed to be out of fashion for about twenty years or more.

His eyeglasses were thick, and they tended to slip down his nose, forcing him to push them back up the slope.

Glenn was not very memorable. Everything was hum-drum, and the question was whether Glenn realized it or not. A hum-drum life and a hum-drum job. In summary, he was rather hum-drum.

He recently downsized to a six-hundred square foot apartment. An apartment in the same complex; just up the road, but it was smaller. He realized that he did not need much space. He had very little in the way of furniture. The manager of the apartment complex came by to check on Glenn after he moved and took note of how even within six-hundred square feet their voices echoed as if they were speaking within a cave. Glenn did not even have any pictures on his walls.

When he was at home, Glenn spent most of his time in a tiny amount of space; about three feet by five feet in his tiny living room. It was there that he had his little "L"-shaped desk, a tiny television sitting on the edge of the one desk, a table radio, and a computer and monitor screen on the other side. One notepad, some pens, and one pencil. He also had a videocassette recorder. From the 1970s. And a collection of videotapes that he picked up at thrift stores in their bargain buckets, and some random on-line shops that sold old goods.

Glenn was single and had no actual friends. His family lived in another state and mostly forgot about him.

But Glenn had Saturday night and that old VCR. And classic movies. And loneliness.

Lonely classic moves.

Every Saturday night, after his chores were complete, Glenn cooked a frozen pizza, he plucked an old video cassette from his collection and he watched a classic movie. It could be from the 40s, the 50s' the 60s, the 70s, the 80s, even the 90s or most any era. But they had to be classics. Classics with classic actors and actresses. Some of those movies he watched ten times or more. Some of them he knew every word and every line. Glenn did not care. It was his weekly highlight.

Saturday night was extra special when he had a new classic to watch! Maybe a new one that he found by chance in that local thrift store. Usually, they were one dollar or less.

Monday morning at the hum-drum job.

"Hey, did you see that new chick in accounting? Oh, baby, she is hot. What a figure! And single. And fresh, and she just moved here. She will need someone to show her around town. I am just the guy for the job." Sly Fox young junior executive at Glenn's job, cooed to a male co-worker with some water cooler talk.

"I saw her first. Bet that I can get a date with her first," the other Sly Fox answered.

"You are on. Two twelve packs on it," Sly Fox One took that bet.

Glenn Willingham walked by and the two junior executives took note of his attire. Glenn wore a suit and a tie with white, blue, and silver stripes that ran across it in haphazard pattern, and shoes that were too tight and they squeaked when he walked. His suit was from the 1980s. Most of his clothes were. His shoes, too. Glenn did not shop for new clothes very often. If ever.

Hum-drum.

"Hey Glenn," Sly Fox One said as he whispered, 'Watch this. This guy is such a dweeb,' to Sly Fox Two, "what did you do this weekend? How about it, did you see that new chickee-poo in accounting? After all, you are a clerk in accounting. For what? Forever?"

Glenn stopped, pushed his eyeglasses up the slope, adjusted his striped tie and answered.

"Fifteen years and three months. My first and only job right out of college. I had a nice weekend. Thank you for asking. Watched 'The Big Sleep' with Humphrey Bogart starring as Philp Marlowe and Lauren Bacall as the love interest. Howard Hawks directed. I did meet the new woman in accounting. Her name is Joyce. Yes. She is very nice. And lovely, too. Have a nice day."

Glenn began to move on, but Sly Fox One's words stopped him as the junior executive asked another question.

"The Big Sleep, huh? Sounds like a big bore." Sly Fox One lowered his voice and said, "Like you are."

"Lovely? Geez, she has a great body! Lovely. Sounds like a typical nerd description!"

Sly Fox Two spouted.

Laughter at Glenn's expense.

Glenn made his way down the hallway. Back to his

hum-drum desk.

"Look! Here she comes!" Sly Fox Two spotted Joyce first and the two junior executives perked up like the Tin Soldiers protecting the Treasure of the Mountain People.

Joyce had overheard the conversation with Glenn.

"Hey there, Joyce," Sly Fox One said as he smiled a plastic smile. "I am. …"

"Not interested. It is not a big bore. It is a classic movie. Wonderful movie. Great novel, too. We call it culture. Classics. Excuse me. I need to fill up my water bottle and get back to work. You two clowns standing here acting like high school kids panting over the new girl in town should take a lesson and do the same. By the way, the Human Resources Department is right down the hall from here. I bet they would love to hear of you actions and comments."

The Sly Foxes scattered. The Tin Soldiers fell like bowling pins hit by a strike.

Joyce filled her bottle up and off she went.

Lunch time.

In the breakroom of the corporate office, Glenn Willingham sat and unfolded his hum-drum sandwich and unpacked his hum-drum lunch box. White American cheese with a slice of turkey on whole wheat bread. A cup of applesauce and a small bag of chips.

Her voice was soft and kind.

"Do you mind if I join you, Glenn?"

Glenn looked up and pushed his eyeglasses up the slope. Joyce's presence shocked him.

Stammering ensued.

"Oh . . . oh. Hello, Joyce. Sure. I mean, no. I mean. . .." Glenn stopped and smiled. "I blew that. Yes. Please do join me, Joyce."

She laughed as she set her lunch down and took the seat next to Glenn.

"Thank you. You should smile often. You have an amazing smile. And cheekbones. Say, do you know what happened to the chauffeur? I heard you talking about 'The Big Sleep' to those two dopes from sales."

Another smile.

"Oh. No. I mean, even Chandler did not know what happened to the chauffeur. It is a legendary plot hole. Do you like classic movies?"

"Love them. They are my thing. Do you really think that I am lovely?"

"Yes. Very much so."

Another smile. He melted her heart when he pushed the eyeglasses up the slope. Glenn had a thought.

"Joyce, every Saturday night, I cook a frozen pizza and watch a classic movie on my VCR. It is my thing. Would you like to. . .."

"Yes! I would love to!"

Hum-drum no more. Glenn moved back to the bigger apartment. He bought a love seat and a modern television with streaming capabilities. Kept the frozen pizza tradition.

Classic movies minus the lonely.

Their wedding picture on the wall kept the echoes down.

Spark Plus

Huff ‘n’ Puff Boss

Fudley was a dedicated employee who worked for a huff ‘n’ puff, and demanding boss.

Huff ‘n’ Boss: “Fudley! Where is the Culver report? It was due on my desk two hours ago! My expectation is results!”

Fudley: “Well, sir. The data is quite complex to sort out. It does take some time.”

Huff ‘n’ Boss: “Time! We don’t have time! Results, Fudley! Results. I must ask you, Fudley. Do you know what you are doing?”

Fudley: “Well, sir. Honestly. If I knew what I was doing, then I wouldn’t be here.”

Spark

Christmas Tree Needle

"There is always that magical moment when Christmas returns. Usually, it is in July when you find that one, last remaining needle from the Christmas tree hidden in a dark corner of the living room floor."

10

Short

Multi-talented Pest Control

The doorbell rang. The woman of the house hustled to open it. It was the monthly pest control service person. Two minutes early.

He stood about as high as he was round. Everything about him was round. Round face. Round body. Round arms and round feet. She wondered how he stood up on round feet.

"Oh, hello. Please come in. You are new. You are two minutes early. What happened to Charlie? He has been coming here for years."

The round man lifted one finger in the air and said, "Two minutes early is better than two minutes late. I pride myself on my timeliness. And my overall efficiency. Pest control is serious business. Pests are home invaders and they require control. To answer your questions, it is my understanding that Charlie resigned. The bugs got the best of him. However, my war with pests continues!"

The round man was quite dramatic. But there was something infectious about him and his positive energy. It was late spring and a little chill remained in the air; the serviceman wore a crisp blue uniform of his company on his round little body, a lightweight jacket over his shirt and a ball cap emblazoned with the company logo on top of his round head. His uniform shirt and the jacket both had the company logo, too. His shirt also had his first name in red stitched embroidery on the left side near a pocket bulging with a pad and a pen.

"Bruce." The stitches announced in red cursive.

He carried a silver tank in his right hand with a wand connected by a hose to the tank. In his left hand, he held a small toolbox. There was a huge flashlight slipped in a belt holder and hugging his round waist.

"Mrs. Stackhouse, I am Bruce Boulder. Now, I spell that like the rock."

Bruce spelled it letter-for-letter. Mrs. Stackhouse nodded. Bruce was a talker and slightly overwhelming.

"I have your service schedule right here and the pest control checklist. I am ready to go and stop pests in their tracks!"

"Okay, well. Thank you for that, Bruce. Come on in. I will show you around and then you can do your thing. I am doing my laundry. . .."

"Oh, yes! Please don't let me interfere. I will find my way and use our comprehensive twenty-seven item service plan to control pests and inspect for any voids and defects in structure that might allow new entries!"

Bruce removed his hat and rolled into the home as if he wore roller-skates. For a round little man; he moved very quickly. Mrs. Stackhouse looked down at his round work shoes just to make sure there were no rollers.

"The kitchen is usually the first place that pests invade and that you notice them. Next, we will inspect the bathrooms, which is the second place we notice pests. The water, you know? Have you seen any activity, Mrs. Stackhouse? Since I assumed Charlie's old route, I must say the pests exhausted him and finally got the best of him, but he was very efficient."

Mrs. Stackhouse stood in the hallway, as Bruce rolled off at fifteen miles-per-hour to the kitchen. She answered.

"No sign of any pests. Usually, we have some ants marching through this time of year from the bay window there in the kitchen . . . but not this year. So far."

Bruce answered from afar as Mrs. Stackhouse could hear him opening and closing cupboard doors.

"I will get them. If they are here! Rest assured!"

Mrs. Stackhouse checked her laundry in the hallway closet and reset the dryer for more drying time. Her curiosity about Bruce's activity led her to the kitchen.

Bruce's round, little body was bulging out of the cupboard underneath the kitchen sink. She could see the light of his flashlight waving all over as he fervently inspected the cabinet. It looked like a spinning disco ball in the center of the dance floor. He looked like a beach ball with legs; but was quite nimble and flexible.

Mrs. Stackhouse said, "Okay. Thank you for your service. Yes. Charlie was very good. Do you know what he is doing now?"

"Sure do! He is instructing skydiving over at the airport. Less stressful than pest control. He jumped in the Army."

Bruce finished his inspection and opened his tool box. He took out small cardboard sticky traps and began setting them out underneath the sink. As he did so, he yapped along.

"Yup. I was in the Navy. Electronics warfare tech. Got out and decided that the ministry called me, so I went off to the priesthood for eight years, but God had different plans for me. A higher calling!"

Mrs. Stackhouse exclaimed, "Oh my! Higher than the priesthood?"

Bruce was off to inspecting the bay window. Down on his hands and knees, intensely poking at the sill with a tool.

"Yup! I became a math teacher in high school. Then a science teacher. Science and pests are very closely related! Study bugs and pests and you know how they operate!"

Mrs. Stackhouse acknowledged the relationship.

"I can see that, yes."

"You have some water intrusion here. Ants love wet wood. Best to have a contractor check the caulking outside."

"Oh. I will let my husband know."

Bruce stood up and said, "Please. Bathrooms? Garage, crawl spaces, and then the attic scuttle. My checklist includes a free spring inspection for bats."

"Oh my. We don't need bats. This way."

"Yes. Never breathe in or try to clean up bat poop, Mrs. Stackhouse. Has some nasty stuff in there. Leave that us professionals."

"I will be sure to note that."

One hour later, Bruce finished. He stood in the main hallway and held his clipboard and pen and yapped once more. Non-stop. Even when he was in the attic, Mrs. Stackhouse could hear him talking.

"All clear, Mrs. Stackhouse. No bats. No pests. Not an invader in sight!"

His round face beamed with the radiance of success. Bruce was very happy.

"I deployed preventative measures, but no direct attacks are necessary at this time. Here, please review my paperwork and if you agree, sign at the bottom. Double-check it because I am dyslexic and tend to make simple errors.”

“Oh, okay. Thank you, Bruce,” she said, taking the clipboard and scanning it. “No, it looks fine. Mrs. Stackhouse signed it and handed it back to Bruce. He smiled. Placed his hat back on his head and rolled to the front door.

Lifting a single finger in the air, and with a flash of zeal in his eyes, Bruce said, “Thank you and we will see you next month! Now, please, Mrs. Stackhouse, if, by chance, you see a single pest, even one ant, please call and I will be out here quick as a flash to stop them in their tracks! I absolutely love my job! I think everyone should be as lucky and as happy as I am!”

He rolled out the door to his truck and disappeared to fight the next battle with bugs and pests.

Mrs. Stackhouse closed the door and leaned up on it while taking a deep breath. Bruce was a pest control dynamo.

The laundry could wait.

She needed a nap.

“So, honey, how was your day?” Mrs. Stackhouse asked her husband as she handed him a glass of wine.

“All the usual. Boring. No one is ever happy. They are all frustrated. Too many numbers not met and too many meetings. Yours?”

“Well, the pest control man came. A new man. He was exceptional in his services. It was just that he talked constantly. It was exhausting.”

“Oh. A talker, huh? What happened to the former guy? I think his name was Charlie. He was coming here for years.”

“Yes. Correct. Charlie. He left to become a skydiving

instructor. The new technician said it was less stressful than pest control is."

Mr. Stackhouse looked at his wife and waved his wine glass in the air in her direction.

With a gentle nod, he asked, "Ha! Seriously? Are you pulling my leg? How much wine have you had, honey?"

Mrs. Stackhouse laughed and confessed.

"Just my second glass. I am serious. No joking. This new guy claimed to have had multiple careers in one lifetime. He was a priest, he served in the Navy, he was a science and math teacher in high school and now he is in pest control. Oh, yes. I almost forgot. And he is dyslexic. And round like a beach ball with legs. His energy was amazing."

She took a long sip of wine. More of a gulp.

"Oh, my. And he is dyslexic? Is that even possible to be a dyslexic teacher and priest? He told you all of this while doing a pest control service call?

"He sure did. Non-stop talking. He was a whirlwind of activity. As far as being dyslexic, well, I am not sure."

"Okay, well. Honestly, he sounds like a nutcase. Do you believe him?"

"Not sure. But I firmly feel as if he believes it and if he does, then more power to him. Oh yes, he passed along a tip. Never breathe in or try to clean up bat poop. Nasty stuff in there."

Her husband almost spit out his wine.

"Do we have bats? My goodness!"

"No bats. All clear. According to Bruce."

"Okay. Great. Well, steering clear of bat poop is something that we will keep in mind but hope that we never encounter. This guy seems very serious."

"Oh, yes. He took the work very seriously. For sure. Yet, he was so happy in his life and work. I guess we all should be so lucky. A valuable lesson learned from the multi-talented pest control guy. Just be happy."

11

Flash!

Splitting the Check

They say that in life that they are firsts, and there are lasts. There also are instant regrets.

She sashayed by like a butterfly working flowers. A flutter of wings, a wave of beauty, a touch of perfume, and every man in the joint allowed their eyes to glance her way. Even the men with their wives, or girlfriends, or others, in their company.

Her floating walk to the restroom, with her beauty on full display, caused some hearts to skip a beat.

The man that she left at the table, of which she shared a meal with, nervously fidgeted. He wondered why this beautiful woman finally accepted his dinner invitation. He had asked her out many times before, and she always turned him down.

She was out of his league. For sure.

It was not that he was totally without appeal. He was tall. Not much else, but tall. She was gorgeous; like a fashion model.

The necklace that she wore around her neck probably cost more than an entire month of his paychecks combined. He was just a clerk in the accounting department and she was an executive assistant to one of the big guns.

He asked her out one more time, despite the past rejections, on a whim of bravery.

The server came by and asked if he wanted another cocktail. For some unknown reason, even though he knew he was over his budget; he answered yes. Instantly, it was an order that he regretted. Not that he was driving. He could walk to his apartment. It was just a few blocks south of here and his date took a taxi.

It was not the alcohol that concerned him; it was the bill. The accounting clerk had suggested they grab coffee; it was her suggestion they come here. To this expensive restaurant. For dinner.

Her reverse trip from the restroom caused the hearts of the male onlookers to skip beats. In reverse. And some female hearts, too. The bartender missed pouring a shot when he looked up to watch the scene. Her long dress waved at her ankles, her hips swayed back and forth like volleys over the net in a tennis match.

When she sat at the table, the server delivered the cocktail and asked, "Ma'am. Did you want one more glass of wine?"

She looked over at her companion and his cocktail and answered without hesitation.

"Of course. Please, make it your best, Merlot. The others were quite good, just a tad too dry."

"Of course," the server replied, "I will be right back."

The accounting clerk intervened before the server retreated and he said, "And please bring the check, too. That *last* wine will close us out."

He wasn't taking any chances on her dialing up any other offerings. He took a large sip of his cocktail. Before the server returned, he asked the question that he needed to ask. He felt emboldened. After all, he simply suggested they enjoy coffee together at the corner coffee shop. It was her suggestion to come here.

"So," he swallowed, took another quick sip of liquid courage, and spoke his thoughts.

"I had a wonderful time. I hope you did so, too. Shall we split the check?"

The server returned. She smiled, thanked them, and placed the glass of wine in front of the woman, then smiled and dropped the billfold containing the check down in front of the accounting clerk. The billfold had elegant designs on the face of it. It was both menacing and welcoming, all in one.

The woman picked the wine up, she swirled the glass, and peered seductively over the rim of it while taking a sip. The accounting clerk could have melted from her beauty.

The woman ignored the first half of his question; instead, she answered the other half.

"Sure. Split it. One of your credit cards in your right hand Another one of your credit cards in your left hand. Ask the server to split them evenly."

She winked seductively over the rim of the glass and added, "I had a lousy time. Last date for us. Never again. Ever."

His heart sank.

They say that in life that they are firsts, and there are lasts. In this case; the first date was also the last date.

There also are instant regrets.

Spark

The Internet

"The Internet. Humankind's best and worst invention."

Spark

Plans

"This was the day that I planned to conquer the entire world. Sadly, it did not happen. Tomorrow is not looking too swift, either. Look out day after the day after the day after tomorrow, here I come!"

12
Short
Christmas Magic in Vernon Valley

The sky rather reluctantly spit out a few snowflakes. It was as if the sky coughed and choked a few frozen blobs of snow that gradually filtered out of the clouds and drifted their way to the ground to settle in wait there. It was an overcast day, slightly foreboding, slightly ominous, very cold, quite frosty, and all together wintry. It was only early December, and it was if the world was already in a deep freeze; beyond being very cold; it made one wonder what January would be like.

The Borough of Haledon, New Jersey, was by no means a bustling town; it was just an enclave tucked between a city and other boroughs of the city of Paterson. A haven of some sorts to escape to on the number fourteen bus. Belmont Avenue was the main thoroughfare, and it had the usual northern New Jersey mix of retail shops, bars, pubs, taverns, and businesses. In fact, the borough had many, many bars, pubs, and taverns. . ..

It was a dark, dull day a few weeks before Christmas in 1978. It was late on a Friday. The snowflakes that spit out of the sky settled upon the sidewalk in a haphazard pattern resembling a sprinkling of talcum powder. When the wind blew, the snow chased across the ground in layers of waves of snow while tumbling gracefully upon each flake and pile before settling in corners and nooks. There, the snow glistened like diamonds, sleeping until the wind disturbed the piles once more.

The locals that lived here forever and a little bit more, always said when the wind blows out of the north, from Wayne to Paterson, across the Preakness Mountains, and it whistles down from High Mountain, then change is on the way. If the wind whistles just before Christmas arrives; then it brings with it a gentle and extra special touch of magic.

It appears as if the local folks were correct.

It was just past five o'clock in the afternoon.

Mr. Alan Francis McClain punched his time ticket out at the clock out at Farber Dye Factory right on time at the stroke of the five o'clock hour. His toolbox weighed a little more than he thought it would and he thought how he should have borrowed a two-wheel handcart from the maintenance shop to lug the tools to his car. The parking lot was large, and he had quite a distance to span to make it to his car. His boss tried very hard to talk him out of leaving; even offered a bump up in salary. Alan refused because it was time. He knew that he was a top-notch maintenance mechanic and the factory would miss his skills on repairing and maintaining the equipment as well as all the issues with the ancient building, yet Alan was tired of smelling like dye and he was sure that the environment might have taken a few years off his life. Breathing in chemicals for twelve years cannot be good for you. Alan did not even want to think about what he had dealt with while serving in the United States Army. The military provided him with some valuable skills, a trade, and some unforgettable experiences. Some were good and most of them were not. Two years active and four years in the reserve. He narrowly avoided combat service in the Vietnam War but he was happy that his military life was over.

Yes, indeed, he had punched his time clock ticket out for the last time. In many ways! He did not know what he was going to do now but he sure as hell knew that he was not going to return to that same old grind come Monday morning. This part of his career was over. Alan needed to get away from here; from the grit and grind of this old borough and the city and noises. He needed fresh air and pine trees, cold, snow, and purity. A new start in the country away from it all.

Yesterday, he put a call in to his old military buddy, Jack Kemp, who lived up in Sussex Couty in New Jersey to see what Jack was doing for the holidays. Alan explained his situation to his old friend. They hit it off in the military when the two of them found out they both were from New Jersey. Although, Sussex County was a far different life than it was in the old city of Paterson and the surrounding boroughs. It was country life! Jack had been a cook in the Army and after serving in the military, Jack opened a restaurant up there in God's country. Just a small place; a country nook and he served up breakfast and lunch, and simple homecooked meals for dinner, along with a very small bar serving, beer, wine, and cocktails. The establishment was small, but very successful. Jack told him to come on up and they could hang out over the holidays. He even offered Alan a gig working in the restaurant until he sorted things out in his life.

"I have a few appliances and other items not working too swift in the kitchen. I am sure you can fix them up and get them back in action in no time," Jack had explained.

In just a few short months, Alan's life took a drastic change. In early November, his wife made the fact that she was moving on in their lives very clear. Their marriage was over. Since she packed her bags and left, Alan's thoughts were all about moving on and finding a new direction in his life. It was too painful to stay here any longer.

People chart their own courses in life and who was he to argue with her decision.

Life between them had grown more and more distant as life went by, and after sixteen years of marriage; she grew bored with their lives and found love elsewhere. Some handsome, young, and wealthy executive in the office where she worked. The guy sure brought a helluva lot more to the table than what Alan did.

Alan lamented, he shed a few tears, reflected on his mistakes, grieved, and then accepted it. Endless overtime and a young, lonely, and beautiful wife lead to straying. He vowed never to work that hard ever again in his life.

Alan McClain set his toolbox down on the sidewalk and turned around to scan the old factory one last time. The smutty windows, the grey finishes, the smokestack looming above the factory reaching up into the wintry mix of clouds and snow. He would not miss the old place. Not one thing about it. In retrospect, Alan would miss some of his co-workers, his boss was a good guy, and he would miss tipping a few cold ones after the Friday late shift over at Hank's Tavern on Belmont Avenue. That was about all he would miss. Not too much else.

Alan McClain picked the toolbox up again, adjusted its position in his hand and he continued on his way to the parking lot. He was out of here. He was just like the snow in the wind on this afternoon; blowing in many directions. Alan made his decision just as he made hers.

Today was payday. Alan had some cash in hand and in his mind, there was no reason to hang around here any longer. The lease was up at the end of December on the apartment over on Cook Street and if he ever was to make a move then the time was now. First came the holidays, and he planned to enjoy the holidays as much as he could do so. Especially so by hanging out with his old military friend. Then, a new year loomed. It was time to turn the negative into the positive.

Alan stepped quickly down the sidewalk alongside of Henry Street and when he realized how cold it was; he set his toolbox down again, and turned his collar up on his overcoat to face the wind and the swirling flakes of snow in the air. He was happy that he tuned in the weather forecast early this morning and tucked his wool hat in his coat pocket before he left the house. The wool felt wonderful perched upon his head and met the snowflakes head-on.

He glanced at his watch. It was now five-ten in the afternoon. His plan was to head to the apartment. Finish packing what he had left to pack. There was no much left. All the furniture was gone now. What his wife did not take, he gave away to charity. He would sleep in his old foldable military cot this weekend. His plans included heading out for some cold beers and a burger for dinner with one last visit to Hank's Tavern before he left for good.

Sunday, he would rest and clean up the apartment for turnover. Come Monday morning, Alan Francis McClain would head for God's country. It was as good a time as any to begin his new life.

He was Debra's life, and she was his. Now Gordon was gone and Debra was empty, desperate, and desolate. She had no idea when he first became seriously ill that he would die so quickly. One moment, her husband was his usual self: vibrant, strong, funny, handsome, sexy, and powerful. The next moment, in what seemed as if it was a blink of the eyes, he withered away; torn-up, worn, and decimated. At first, the doctors were optimistic and then they were vague, and then they were downcast, and then they pronounced the truth.

Then . . . Gordon was gone. Debra held his hand as he took his last breath.

Debra did not know here to turn or where her next decision would come from; after all, owning and operating the Vernon Valley Inn was her husband's dream. Not her dream.

His family, his heritage, his history. Not hers. The inn had been the family's business for over forty years. Yet, she felt the honor, the obligation, the courage, the motivation of it all. Debra knew it was much more than just bricks, and wood, and windows, and rooms, and keys, and cement, and carpet, and landscaping and ski slopes and . . . the Christmas tree in the lobby of the Vernon Valley Inn. A tree that Gordon dragged out of the depths of the storage confines of the inn every year set in place and he decorated to the hilt, despite Debra proclaiming that the tree had seen better days and required replacement. She could still see his smile after he finished decorating the tree.

Then, he stood back and admired it with his hands on his hips, he tilted his head one way, then another and then with the classic display of humor that he always had, he looked upside down at the tree with his head looking between his legs and proudly proclaimed, "There! Perfect! Fantastic!"

Gordon Winston had a marvelous sense of humor. He could always make her laugh; even if she was tired and grumpy. Gordon had a special magic about him.

My goodness, she missed him and it seemed as his passing in the spring of this same year was just a few weeks ago. He was her lover, her husband, and her best friend. Nothing seemed the same. Nothing. She could smell his manly scent in their closet, on his clothes that still hung in the bedroom closets and in their bed.

Now with only a few weeks until Christmas, and the ski resort just a few miles down the road, and the business booming, Debra had little time to grieve. It was such a difficult time. Christmas can bring so much joy, but it also brings the pain of the loss of loved ones, of memories of times long since gone from our lives. Her duty was to keep the dream alive. Her mission was to keep the inn operating in his honor and hold this all together.

Somehow.

However, how exactly did Debra go about doing that? So much had happened since his passing. She had no formal training in this business; she learned by attrition from watching her husband for five years, but how she wished that she had devoted more attention to how the business operated. Right now, the economy was not the best; but not the worst it had been. Employees were difficult to find here in Sussex County; most commuted to the lower and more populous counties down Route 23 and earned higher wages than the hospitality business could pay. A few holdover employees remained from the old days. Some of the housekeepers remained, a few of the desk clerks stayed along with one of the night auditors who had been with the business since when Gordon's father operated the inn and the related businesses. Good old Andrew Gleason was as reliable as the sunset and the sunrise. Daily, Debra made sure that she thanked him for his reliability, loyalty, and his efforts. Debra prayed and thanked God every day for Andrew Gleason, but she had to be realistic. Andrew was seventy-three years old, and soon, he would retire and end a long career. It seemed as if it was a collision of every world that Debra could ever imagine.

The troublesome situations were seemingly endless. First, the loss of her husband and then with the leaving of the inn's chief engineer, Mr. Chris Robinson, the maintenance and operation of the property and facilities of the inn became a huge concern. When Chris left, he took all the secrets of how to operate and maintain the building and grounds with him. The Vernon Valley Inn operated at a high standard of quality, and the facilities were a large part of the experience. Her husband's family and Gordon always maintained the facility to the highest standard. The housekeeping was always top-notch and the facilities, landscaping, and every aspect of the building and grounds were always pristine. Mr. Chris Robinson was a large part of the operation and his skills and dedication explained the outstanding maintenance and perfect appearance and operation of the facilities and property. His skills were amazing; a former Navy maintenance mechanic onboard a large aircraft carrier, there was nothing the man could not fix or operate. Gordon's father hired him twenty or so years earlier. Chris stayed on all these years until his parents aged and required assistance and illness crept in with their old age. Chris was their only child, and he had to take care of his family. She understood and knew it was inevitable that Chris would need to leave and take care of his parents. The last few months that he worked, emergencies often occurred with his parents that took him away from work. Then finally, he had to relocate to where his parents lived in southern New Jersey to take care of his family and personally attend to the matters. He generously accepted her phone calls and provided guidance and advice as he that he could; however, Debra did not want to take advantage of his kindness at a time of a family crisis, she only called him when she had no alternatives and was desperate for his assistance.

Now, she called in outside contractors for most every repair and situation and it was costing the inn a fortune. The job ad for a new chief engineer yielded very few job applicants. The few that did apply wanted a higher wage than Debra could afford to provide or they were not qualified or had other issues.

Debra had spent a barrel full of money on job ads and now, in a sign of futility or surrender, she resorted to putting a help wanted sign out on the entrance to the inn and a detailed job posting on a little corkboard on an easel at the front desk. The signs had generated no leads or interest so far; but at least Debra was not spending a fortune on job advertisements.

The next adverse blow to the situation was when old Danny Salisbury and his wife decided to retire from running the restaurant adjacent to the inn. They were off to Florida for a well-deserved retirement. They too, had been with the inn for a very long time, since Gordon's father operated the inn, and while the restaurant was technically, a separate business entity that the Salisbury family owned and operated, and paid rent for the building, the two businesses were vital to each other's success. That fact had caused some previously loyal guests and customers to look elsewhere for lodging this season, because the convenience of the food and drink next to the inn was an unbeatable selling point. Guests found it most enjoyable after a long day on the slopes to settle in and not have to venture back out in the snow and ice and cold for meals.

Sure, the area had other eateries and restaurants nearby the resort and slopes, but having the attached restaurant right next door to the inn, where the guests could simply walk down a connecting hallway to enjoy fine food and drinks; was a main attraction for staying at the Vernon Valley Inn. Furthermore, the restaurant served an upscale variety of food and drink that was a step above what was available elsewhere in the area. This fit the niche of the pricing of the inn, which was a little more than the other lodging charged in the area. Far and wide, people visiting the area knew that the Vernon Valley Inn had a fine reputation for being a wonderful place to enjoy a winter holiday break, a Christmas getaway or otherwise. Recently Vernon Valley was working to become a four-season resort area—not just a ski resort.

Debra now owned an empty restaurant building, too. A building that required maintenance and upkeep, and utilities and taxes to pay; not to mention how it hurt the inn's business. She had a local realtor working hard to lease the empty restaurant, and the local Chamber of Commerce and business organizations working hard to identify a new restaurateur to take over the business, but so far, there was very little interest.

Debra needed to fulfill or change the motto on the business card and all the advertisements for the inn, where it stated the adjacent restaurant served up the finest of food and drink. There were none available at the inn right now. It was just another item to cause Debra angst, worry, and cause her to wonder how much longer she could sustain the dream that Gordon so dearly wanted. They never had any children; the inn was their child, and it pained Debra to think that she was going to fail in the mission to keep Gordon's dream and legacy alive now that he was gone.

It was Monday morning and Christmas loomed closer and closer every day. Despite the lack of a restaurant, it had been a busy weekend at the Vernon Valley Inn. The snowmaking on the slopes earlier in the month hit the news and the local ski reports of open slopes so close to the metro-New York City and Northern New Jersey area had sent local skiers into a winter frenzy. Then, to top it off, the area had a ten-inch snowfall beginning on Friday night and carrying on into Saturday afternoon. That fresh powder sent even more skiers trekking up Route 23 for some early season fun. Then, after a short lapse in natural snowfall, another snowfall was moving in on Monday. Natural snow on an already thick base of snow meant skiers were going to come in abundance! And then, in a few short weeks, the peak Christmas holiday season arrives.

The skiers would arrive; despite any snow on the roads or obstacles. Hamburg Mountain loomed in majesty and in its foreboding nature. As picturesque as it was, the mountain also was rather treacherous to traverse. Hamburg Mountain and its winding sections of Route 23 connected the lower metro areas to the Vernon Valley. The mountain had a way of humbling the best of drivers, both in summer and in winter. Under snowy conditions, the roadways over the mountain were extra tricky. The locals knew of its winding ways, and they respected it; even with the best four-wheel-drive vehicles. The mountain had little mercy during the wintertime. When faced with the prospect of navigating the treacherous mountain road to head back down to the valleys of Pequannock and Wayne Township, many skiers decided to ride out the storm and leave late Sunday night or early Monday morning after the road maintenance crews could clear the roadways over the mountain.

The weekend's business and activities exhausted Debra. She was short-handed on the housekeeping staff as well as in the laundry department, and she had to turn some rooms over herself and clean them on her own. She could have done without the party guys smoking weed in room seventeen and forcing her to drag the ozone machine out to kill the smell, but they were polite and tipped very well! Besides, she recalled being young and adventurous once.

Now, early Monday morning checkouts were over. It was close to noon and Debra had worked the front desk until Andrew Gleason relieved her. Good old Andrew. Even at seventy-three years of age, Andrew was still her best employee, and he came in this morning to swing an additional shift to take the pressure off Debra. Andrew Gleason was a godsend. Tall, lean, magnificent blue eyes and a gentle swirl of white hair that framed his handsome features; and an even smile and wise crinkles of wisdom surrounding his blue eyes. Even at his age, he could turn some women's heads. Debra imagined when he was young; he sure had his pick of the young women! He was a widower, maybe even now he does! All Debra knew was that she loved him!

Debra ran over the remaining schedule and relayed that the rest of the day should be light, and finally, after Andrew settled in, she had a chance to take a break. In the restroom, she stared at her image in the mirror. She splashed some water on her face, blinked and deeply sighed. Debra was only forty years old, and right now, she felt as if she was eighty. She studied her face, and she looked a wreck. Her eyes sunk deep into her head, the wrinkles around her mouth were deep and she never wore make-up anymore. Why even bother? Every day was the same!

She never ate very well these days, nor did exercise anymore, nor did she take good care of herself; yet her weight loss was marginal, yet twisting and turning in front of the mirror in the restroom, Debra felt her figure still held its own. Her breasts were small but perky, her stomach slim, her hips okay. Debra had never given a thought to romance after she lost her precious Gordon. If romance did come her way, where would it even come from these days? A social life and romance were the farthest thing from her mind right now because she just needed some rest and respite.

Where did she ever dream that rest and respite would come from? Especially now, with the busiest time of the year rapidly approaching. And she needed the business, the maximum revenue, the dollars, the cents, the bedlam. Debra leaned her head into the mirror. The tears that she previously resisted made their way to her eyes and without any barriers, the tears broke through and they streamed down her face. She could no longer withstand them. The tears won this battle.

With her head in her hands, while rested upon the mirror, Debra Winston cried out, "Lord, please give me strength to continue."

All she wanted was to calm and silence the noises in her head. She was desperate.

When everything seems lost and we cry in desperation, compassion settles in. Be it from God, or from Heaven above, or from the depths of a spiritual world where we do not know or understand; it arrives. Compassion settles in and help arrives on waves of love.

Debra glanced at her watch. Now, she needed to figure out the next few hours and try to keep the business, her emotions and everything else in her life on the rails and hope that she could do so without any derailments!

Mr. Alan Francis McClain steered his old sedan along the winding road of Route 94 and he carefully followed what he could see of the centerline of the roadway and the line for the shoulder of the road. The snow had started to fall when he hit Butler Township on Route 23, and now it grew fierce in intensity. He was sure glad he made it over that huge mountain before the snow fell as heavily as was falling right now. His big old sedan had studded snow tires, he had his heavy tool chest, and some sandbags in the trunk for added weight over the wheels, and a snow shovel just in case he slipped off the roadway and fell into a drift of snow or two, but that mountain was the real deal. Alan wondered how in the world residents that live up here made that journey to what was surely more lucrative jobs and opportunities on the other side of the mountain in the counties closer to New York City, or in fact, in the big city itself.

'They sure are hardy and sturdy folks here in Sussex County. Or perhaps, on snow days, they just stayed home rather than battle the treacherous Hamburg Mountain roadway,' Alan thought as he leaned in a little closer to the windshield to study the roadway. He glanced to the side to try to catch a house number or street number on one or two of the businesses that lined the roadway, but it was futile. He had never been to Jack's restaurant or his house before, so this was new territory for him. The snow was falling too heavily right now to see very far, and the wind picked up a little more and blew the snowflakes in great waves. Alan glided to a stop at a red traffic light and watched as his windshield wipers cleaned the snow from the glass in noisy thumps as the rubber battled the clumpy snow. Alan watched a huge snowplow truck glide to a stop in the opposite lane from where he sat. Alan thought how the road crews did a wonderful job keeping up on the roadways around these parts to keep the flow of travelers, skiers, and other winter lovers, safely rolling along to the ski resort that Alan hoped was just down the road. The resort was a popular attraction, being the closest major ski resort to the big city, and the populated counties of northern New Jersey down on the other side of Hamburg Mountain. The resort was an important moneymaker for the local businesses, and tax revenue for the county. Many local businesses, such as Jack's restaurant, counted on the attraction and the revenue granted by a snowy winter season and the skiers and winter enthusiasts who would flock to the area to enjoy it. From what Alan knew of it, Jack's restaurant, known simply as "The Hutch" was a small operation but successful.

The traffic light turned green, Alan tapped the gas pedal a little, the studded tires easily gripped the asphalt surfaces underneath the layers of snow, and the big sedan rolled forward slowly. Traffic slowly crawled along, but the snowplows had been down this side of the road and the snow cover was greasy but not too deep.

So, here he was, rolling through the snow searching for The Hutch at six hundred, Route 94, with everything that he owned packed in the large sedan. He did not own much. All he had left were sparse indicators of his past life; he had some family heirlooms, some pots and pans, knives and forks, and beer mugs and some drinking glasses, his clothes, his military cot, and, of course, his tools. Alan was happy to leave it behind; and he planned to enjoy this

Christmas. What was not to enjoy? It was snowing; he was in the country, a ski resort, and a quaint, picturesque little village far from the gritty city and tucked in a snowy valley.

A Christmas picture postcard.

No doubt that Alan always loved Christmas. From when he was a little boy until now. He loved the festive feelings of the Christmastime of the year. The glow of Christmas lights on a tree or in a store window that turned everything into a holiday fairyland. He enjoyed the music of the season, and most of all, Alan enjoyed how even the grumpiest and nastiest people of the world had a little spring in their step and wore an occasional smile, too. Moreover, he sure loved the winter, so here he was. Alan remained determined, despite the sad and uneven circumstances, to make this Christmas a joyful and festive time.

The road turned a little sharper at a bend in the road and Alan let up on the gas and eased the sedan into the turn. He was a very good driver in the snow and handled the turn without slipping or sliding. There, on the other side of the bend in the roadway, through the snowflakes whipping around, Alan spotted a roadside sign proclaiming the arrival of the ski resort, "Only three miles up the road."

No sooner than he could mumble, "Jack's place must be getting very close now," something caught his eye, peeking out of the heavy snowfall. It was a large facility. Maybe a hotel or a motel. A sign stood proudly out front near the entrance to the facility's parking lot; a sign elegantly detailed in handsome script letters with a logo of a snowy valley with skiers on a mountain and on each side of the sign were large matching lantern lights that glowed orange through the snowfall and lit up the sign magnificently.

"The Vernon Valley Inn," the sign proclaimed.

"Ah ha! The Vernon Valley Inn. It *is* a hotel. Seems like a fancy kind of joint. Might be a good place to stop and ask for directions rather than wander any farther down this snowy road. Maybe I already drove past Jack's place and missed it in the snow," Alan mumbled aloud as he flipped his turn signal on, slowed and eased into the turn to enter the driveway leading to the parking lot. The cars following behind Alan slowed and then when Alan's sedan ventured off the main roadway, they carefully passed and they made their way down the roadway through the snow and to wherever this snowy day was going to bring them.

When Alan's car glided by the entrance sign, it was then that he noticed the plastic sign stuck in the snow, snow covered, just barely poking above the accumulating snow, but it remained readable. "Help Wanted" proclaimed the sign, in bright orange letters on a black background. Alan shook his head a little at the coincidence of the fact that right now, he technically was unemployed. He allowed his mind to wander as to what types of positions were open at the inn. While cruising slowly over the snow-covered asphalt, Alan searched for a parking spot in the large lot. The parking lot had quite a few empty spaces; but Alan figured that was because of weekend checkouts. He imagined that with this new snow falling, the lot and hotel would fill up quickly with skiers joyfully heading for the slopes. It was Monday morning, but that did not matter when it was snowing heavily and Christmas loomed. Begin the holiday early and take advantage of the winter weather.

Being a building and facility maintenance person, who focused his attention on the operational details of properties, Alan noticed that no snowplows made their way through the parking lot just yet; no doubt, Alan thought, 'The maintenance crew for the inn was waiting for the snow to accumulate a little deeper before beginning snow removal operations. No sense in wasting gas and labor now; the prediction was for the snow to fall all day and into the evening hours before tapering off to snow flurries.'

By the time that the storm would end, it might be a foot of snow for these parts. Alan recalled the local radio station that he tuned into on his car's radio, predicted about a foot of new snow. And that was at least a half an hour or so ago. Just when Alan made it over Hamburg Mountain.

Mr. Alan McClain knew snow removal techniques from his time on the maintenance crew at the factory. His foreman at the factory always put Alan in charge of the snow removal operations. The parking lot for the factory was huge, and the sidewalks wrapped around the factory on three sides. Then there were the loading docks, too! Snow removal in loading docks was a tricky undertaking. It was a major project, yet Alan always enjoyed the snow removal operations. He always felt as if he required more of that fresh clean air to clear his body of those nasty chemicals.

Alan found an open parking spot in one of the closest rows to the front door of the inn. He pulled into the spot, shut off the engine and stared at the landscape, the lot, and the buildings in front of him. The inn and property were both quite large, and the facility was impressive.

It was a gorgeous sprawling property that even under snow cover, Alan could tell that the management kept the property well maintained and groomed. Glorious pine trees stood with the beauty of snow draped upon their tips and stuck to the structure of their trunks while they stood majestically around the property. The rear of the property backed right up to the ski resort and the slopes. You could see the light towers of the resort glowing, and the ski lifts and the cables of the system even through the snowfall carrying happy skiers up the slopes.

As far as the inn's appearance, Alan was keen to the fact that the actual architecture resembled a ski chalet. A ski chalet in New Jersey! Alan found it fascinating! The entrance to the inn had trim and posts and overhangs of rustic timbers and it had large interesting front windows, brightly glowing in multi-colors of Christmas lights. The lobby entrance roof had Christmas lights tacked to the edges, and it outlined the roof edges in a Christmas glow. It was gorgeous, and Alan admired every aspect of the building. Certainly, as far as curb appeal goes, it was a far cry from the gloomy chemical factory that he worked in and maintained for all those years. The lodging section of the inn towered above the grand lobby entrance, and it appeared as if each room had individual decks and overhangs for each room. Because he was a facility maintenance professional, Alan, in admiration of the structure, studied every aspect of this facility. He stopped and counted each level of the building.

Alan mumbled aloud, "Three stories high. Must be at least two-hundred rooms here."

Attached to the right side of the inn was another building. A restaurant, but it was not open right now. In fact, it appeared closed. As in permanently closed. A "For Lease" sign stood out in front of the entrance to the restaurant. In a few of the windows, there were other signs announcing, and advertising, a "Business Opportunity" with a real estate agent's contact information printed upon them. Perched above the front entrance, there were signs of the recent removal of a sign on the banner board of the structure. Alan surmised that the restaurant recently closed, and he thought how that was unfortunate. To have this large of a lodging establishment and not to have a restaurant for dining with quality food and drinks must be affecting the inn's business adversely. Alan wondered what the circumstances were behind the restaurant's closing were.

"Okay, let's pop in here and ask for directions. I bet with this restaurant here closed, the front desk will know where Jack's place is," Alan spoke aloud.

He grabbed his hat from the passenger's seat, zipped his vest up tightly around his neck, and he clamped the wool hat down tightly on his head. Alan forcibly grabbed the handle to the driver's door and yanked it open to step out on the snowy asphalt and make his way to the front door of the lobby.

Alan thought how the gentleman shoveling the snow in front of the entrance to the inn might not have picked to wear a suit and tie to shovel snow, and in fact, he might be a little too old to be out here in the cold, shoveling the snow off the sidewalks and addressing any ice accumulations. The man was tall, maybe as tall as Alan was, and he looked lean, but he was not wearing boots and wore only a hat to fight the cold and snow. No overcoat or vest or other outer garments; only his business attire. Alan stood there watching the man scrape the snow from the walkway with his tie waving in the wind and his hat perched sideways on his head, accumulating some snow on top of it while he worked. He surmised that he was the front desk clerk of the inn and he had grabbed the shovel to make the entrance safe for pedestrians and the guests.

"I think you need to leave that to the maintenance crew," Alan McClain commented as he pointed at the snow and ice on the front sidewalk. "You need some winter clothes there, sir. Ya gonna catch a chill."

The tall man in the suit and tie looked up and smiled as he adjusted the hat on his head, and realizing that it was full of snow, he removed it, shook the snow off and then plopped it back upon his head. Alan noted how he had a thick head of white hair and a genuine smile.

Alan thought, 'This elderly man was very professional and impressive in his appearance.'

He explained the situation.

"Well, I could leave it for the maintenance crew, if only for one major reason. Right now, we don't have any. I guess I am the front desk clerk and the maintenance person, too. We must use an outside landscape contractor for snow removal and that does not always work out so well. They eventually get around to taking care of our maintenance needs here, but we are on a long list with others. There is a snowplow truck in the maintenance shop here and a snow blower and all kinds of equipment . . . but no one to operate them."

The man gave one or two more scrapes of the snow at the sidewalk, then grabbed his shovel, and pointed at the front door of the inn and said, "Anyway. I did not mean to share sad laments with you, sir. Please! Come in! Welcome to the Vernon Valley Inn. I am, Mr. Andrew Gleason. Are you checking in?"

Mr. Alan McClain stood watching Andrew and he tried hard to recover from Andrew's proclamation of there not being any maintenance crew. An inn this large, this dynamic, all the moving parts and pieces, not to mention snowstorms, and no in-house maintenance crew? Alan knew buildings and the business well enough to know that was a recipe for disaster. He connected the dots with the help wanted sign out at the front entrance; the inn was looking for a facilities maintenance person. Andrew waved to the front door; he pulled it open and held it for Alan. Recovering from his thoughts, Alan weakly nodded in Andrew's direction and he walked into the lobby of the inn.

Alan found some words as he followed Andrew into the

lobby.

As his eyes darted around the interior of the lobby, Alan said, "Ah, no. Sorry to bother you. I am not checking in here. I was hoping for some directions. I am trying to find an old military buddy of mine's home and his restaurant. I am spending Christmas with him and hanging out for the holidays. He needs some work done on his restaurant and equipment, so I am going to do some repairs and maintenance for him while I am visiting. The snow is heavy now, I am not familiar with the area and I think I drove past it. Apparently, his home is next to his restaurant business."

Just as Alan studied the exterior of the facility, he also studied the interior, too. The lobby, just as the exterior was, announced hospitality and it, too, was remarkable in appearance. The rustic timber structure of the chalet-styled architecture continued as the ceiling arched high above the lobby to the roof peaks. A rustic deck wrapped around the perimeter of the lobby above the front desk and sitting area in the lobby. Along the timber railings, holiday wreaths of fresh evergreens hung, and they twinkled with dainty holiday lights. Alan could see that the deck and overhangs led to the entrances to the guest rooms and he could see the elevator's doors opened out onto the deck areas. The lobby had a magnificent Christmas tree standing in a corner next to an elegant fireplace, a fireplace where a wood fire glowed in gold and yellow and blue embers behind the fireplace safety screens. Alan enjoyed hearing the pops and crackle of the logs in the fireplace. Not to mention that the wood burning smell was captivating! The lobby walls were full of rustic art, with ski resorts and winter sports depicted, local photography of famous landmarks and even a most recognizable photograph that Alan knew very well. A beautiful photograph of The Great Falls of Paterson, New Jersey. Everything was perfect; the inn and resort area was a holiday getaway that broadcasted Christmas, winter, fun in the snow and even romance. Yes, it was a romantic place and he could see how couples could lose themselves here very easily in the Christmas magic.

Andrew was standing behind the front desk. From there, the old desk clerk carefully studied Alan. Mr. Andrew Gleason recognized the fact that Alan was smiling widely in a display of how he was awestruck at the wonderful lobby, and the decorations, and the aura it presented. Alan Francis McClain was falling in love with the facility and the property and the magic all around him.

Andrew caught Alan's vibe of admiration.

"Ah yes. It is magnificent, isn't it? Such a wonderful place. And the owner, Mrs. Winston, outdid herself this year. It is extra . . . special. Everyone has the same reaction whenever they first see and admire it. Me too and I have been working here for a very long time. I love this time of the year. The snow makes it extra special. A little extra work but it is special to have snow at Christmastime. You are not bothering me. In fact, you gave me an excuse to come inside and warm up a bit. So . . . directions. Yes. Your buddy? A military buddy. What is the name of the restaurant? There are quite a few up and down ninety-four. How can I help you?"

Suddenly, finding Jack's place found a place in the back of his mind. This lobby and the facility and the fact that they required help in the maintenance department took over his thoughts.

Alan smiled and his eyes continued to wander around the lobby while he slowly walked over to the front desk.

Alan said, "Ah, yes, it is breathtakingly beautiful. Perfect for Christmas. In fact, it is perfect for any day or season. Ah, well, my buddy's name is Jack Kemp. He owns The Hutch restaurant."

"Oh yes! Jack is a great guy! We know him well and he serves up wonderful food. You are military friends. That makes sense. Jack told me that he cooked in the Army. Unfortunately, our own restaurant closed here with the owners retiring and moving on with their lives. It had been very successful, too. Such a shame. Especially so, now at our peak holiday season and the ski resort open and generous snowfalls. We are searching for new owners and business partners to reopen it. However; in the meantime, when guests ask for food, drink, and dining suggestions, The Hutch is always on our suggestion list. It is a small place, only a few tables, so it fills up fast, but great service and Jack's home cooking is legendary. I bet it is a lot better than Army chow was."

Andrew chuckled at his own statement and Alan agreed and laughed along with him.

"I bet. Half the time, I could not even figure out what I was eating in the Army."

Alan immediately liked Mr. Andrew Gleason. He was warm, wholesome, and exactly the kind of employee that an inn such as this was would need working the front desk. He was an ambassador.

Andrew kindly explained and provided the directions.

"Well, I assure you that The Hutch does not serve any military chow. Yes. I am afraid you drove by Jack's place. The snow is heavy right now and it might be difficult to see. You will need to turn around and head back south on route ninety-four. It is about a half-mile down the road. Just past a small medical building that has a large blue sign out front. That sign you cannot miss. They light it up when it is dark outside. Vernon Medical Care is on the blue sign. Jack's place is just to the side of the medical building. Tucked a little farther back. His home is next door. That is how it goes in these parts. We are still mostly rural here in

Sussex County. Route ninety-four is where it is at. This roadway has most of the retail establishments, various services, and lodging and restaurants around here, along with the ski resort and winter activities."

Alan's mind was whirling and his original purpose for this snowy mission was now no longer his primary mission. For some reason; a reason that he could not exactly pinpoint as to why, other than the proverbial gut feeling, he felt drawn to this place.

And the help wanted sign called to him.

Andrew Gleason had spent a lifetime interacting with people. Day after day. Month after month. A lifetime of experience. He would acquaint himself with people within a few short minutes of interaction over a hotel front desk check-in process. Andrew could read people and their body language better than a homicide detective or criminal prosecutor could. Andrew studied Alan McClain and he could sense that there was something else on his mind.

"Did that help you, sir? The Hutch is just down the road. Even in the snow . . . just look for the blue sign. Or is there something else that I might assist you with?"

Andrew probed with his questions.

Mr. Alan McClain responded, but his words amplified his wandering mind.

"Ah, yeah. Ha! Oh well. I missed it in the snow. Must have cruised right by it, but it is coming down out there like crazy. Difficult to see out the windshield and the side windows. Thank you so much for the information and directions. I will back track. Have to ask you, though, Andrew, I am curious about the help wanted sign and the fact that you were shoveling the sidewalk because you have no maintenance crew. I mean . . . what openings are available? While walking in, I saw the help wanted sign out there at the front entrance to the parking lot. What or who you are looking for?"

Andrew's eyes lit up, and he studied Mr. Alan McClain. Tall, sturdy, big hands, muscular, a thick head of neatly trimmed and groomed black hair, a whisper of stubble on his face, bright brown eyes, a very handsome man who certainly appeared as if he was not afraid of working. A heavy New Jersey accent but well spoken, too.

Andrew sensed the moment. He explained.

"Well, yes, we have a chief engineer position open. Right there on the desk is the job posting. We have had the opening for a long time. Our long-time head of maintenance retired and moved away, and it has been a struggle to fill the opening with a qualified person. Honestly, we are sort of desperate now. Maintenance is one of the most important functions of an inn such as this. It never stops—only becomes worse when you put off repairs. Of course, now is the super-busy season. You mentioned that you were going to help your buddy Jack out with some repairs at his place. It seems as if you have skills. I mean, ah, do you have any experience?"

Alan chuckled and said, "Well, yes. Yes, I do. Yes, I am planning on helping my buddy with some repairs that he needs. As well as hang out and enjoy Christmas and the holidays with an old friend. I have many, many years of experience. Many years. Both military and civilian." Alan stared at Andrew, smiled, and said, "Honestly, there isn't too much that I can't fix or maintain." He turned and pointed to the front door of the inn and laughed while saying, "I am really good at snow removal, too." Alan then walked over to the desk and leaned in to read the job posting on the little easel sitting there on the counter. He read every word, and he knew there was nothing here that he could not do, and do very well, too. He was more than qualified for the position.

Alan felt wonderful, he felt enlivened, and born anew. Whatever it was that was happening, Alan's confidence that it was the right place and the right time in his life remained high. Alan had a feeling this amazing inn in the country was going to be a very good place for his life. After what he experienced recently in his life, this was exactly what he required. The facility and the property were gorgeous, it seemed like an adequate challenge for his skills, and as for starting anew, this sure fit that requirement.

Alan's exuberance bubbled over.

After reading the job description, Alan stood up and said, "Thank you, sir, for pointing this out to me. I am very well qualified for this opening. It is a huge coincidence or maybe fate, but it just so happens that I am actively looking for a new job. I don't have a resume yet, just left my long-time job a few days ago. In fact, last Friday. I am looking to start anew, which was another reason as to why I came up to visit Jack. Help him out and enjoy the holidays. Clear my mind with some clear air. I would like to fill out an application and receive some consideration for the opening. It would be best if I called Jack and explained and if I get the job, then I might need to break away and fix some things for him, but other than that, I can start right away. That fact might bring me some favor in consideration for the position. In fact, right now. Mr. Andrew Gleason, thank you. Nice to meet you. I am Alan Francis McClain."

Alan stuck his hand out, Andrew Gleason grabbed it, and the two men enthusiastically shook hands.

"Oh boy, it is my pleasure to meet you, Mr. McClain. My pleasure for sure! Please call me, Andrew. Let me grab an application."

Andrew Gleason nodded emphatically; he smiled widely and hurried over to a drawer behind the front desk and opened it, and pulled a job application out from within the pile of papers inside. Andrew's enthusiasm at the prospect of filling the opening was obvious.

"Did you want to call Jack Kemp and explain the situation? He might be worried about you. With the snowstorm and all."

"Good idea. That would be great, Andrew. May I use that phone over there on the table?"

Andrew nodded and said, "Yes, yes, of course. It is a local call. Just dial the number nine first and then the number. In the meantime, here is a job application and a pen. Once you finish with the call, then please, sit down over there in the chair in front of the fireplace, catch some magical warmth from the flames and complete it. I will let Mrs. Winston know that you are here. She might be available to interview you right away."

"Thank you, Andrew. Please call me, Alan. Ah, yes. Mrs. Winston. You mentioned her before. I guess she is the owner of the inn?"

"That's right. Yes, Mrs. Debra Winston. I will be right back."

Alan took the application, walked over to the table, and took a piece of paper out of his wallet with Jack's telephone number on it. He dialed Jack up and his old buddy answered on the second ring.

"Hey, Jack. Alan here. I figured I better give you a call. You might have figured that I ran off the road somewhere and needed a rescue mission."

Jack was a little breathless, but happy to hear from his friend.

"Well, Bud, it did cross my mind, but honestly, we are

so busy here with skiers, I had not had a break to worry too much. I know you are strong and quite capable. Where you at?"

Alan chuckled as he said, "Well, right down the road from you. I rolled by your place in the snow and missed it. Wandered into this place called the Vernon Valley Inn and now. . .."

Alan went on and explained the situation to his friend.

"I know you are busy. Don't want to keep you, but I will come by once I finish up here. I promised to help you out and I will, even if I get this position."

"Hey, Bud. It is all good. Sometimes fate pushes you to certain places for a reason. You've really been through the mud as of late. Really hard times. It is Christmas. Time for some holiday joy and magic! Truly, I hope it works out for you. That is a super cool place there. Debra and Andrew are top-notch. She needs the help bad. She is a great gal. Her husband passed a little while back. In the spring of this year. She is trying to run that joint on her own. Real sad situation. Hey, it is all good. I wish you the best of luck there with that potential job. I will see you soon. Right now, I have to get back to the grille. Super busy in here, today. The skiers are hungry!"

"Sure. Be by soon. Thanks, Jack."

Alan ended the call. He sat near the fireplace and began to fill out the job application while Andrew Gleason hustled off to what Alan assumed were the management offices for the inn, in the section behind the front desk, underneath the deck and overhangs.

Andrew gently tapped on the open door to Debra's office and she turned to see him smiling widely and broadly at her as he stood in the doorway. Debra Winston could not withstand smiling in return. She placed her pen down to mark the spot in her general ledger. There was a table radio sitting on her desk that was softly playing some Christmas music broadcasting from the local radio station, and when she saw Andrew, Debra leaned in and turned down the volume on the radio.

"I was trying my best to feel the Christmas spirit while keeping an ear to the weather forecast. At least twelve inches of the white stuff heading our way, Andrew. Maybe even more. Great for business, bad for us with no help. Going to be an adventure clearing the lots and sidewalks. Thank you for clearing the front entrance. I will ditch my hippie leather boots here and get my snow boots on and my hat and coat and do what I can in a few minutes. My goodness, Andrew. You look so happy and radiant. What has you smiling so widely and handsomely? Did you win the lottery?"

Andrew laughed, waved, and proclaimed, "Nope! Way better! We actually have a job applicant for the chief engineer's position. Tall, muscular, polite, well-spoken, neatly groomed, claims to have many years of experience both in the military and in the civilian world, too. Claims to be able to fix anything and he is an expert in snow removal. And," Andrew winked and smiled again while adding, "he is a very handsome guy, too. Mr. Alan Francis McClain. He is filling out the job application right now. By the fireplace. And get this, he can start right away. As in right now. A foot or more of snow! Who cares?"

Debra shook her head to knock the cobwebs out and to make sure she heard Andrew correctly. Her words came out haltingly to reflect her shock and surprise at the situation.

"Ah, ah, really? Wow! My goodness. No wonder you are smiling! I mean, where did he come from, Andrew?"

"He said he was driving down Route 94 to come up and

visit his friend from the military. He is friends with Jack Kemp. The owner of The Hutch. He promised Jack to repair some items for him at his restaurant and his home and then hang out together over Christmas. He got lost in the snow and drove by Jack's place and he stopped here to ask for directions. He saw me shoveling the front sidewalk, and we chatted and I told him about the job opening and how we currently do not have any maintenance persons. He saw the help wanted sign. Apparently, Mr. McClain just left his job a few days ago and is looking for a new job. He is not some fly-by-night vagabond, Debra. This guy is the real deal. A straight-up military man. Disciplined. I can tell. Can you interview him now? I kind of, and sort of, mentioned that you might be able to do so. I also might have let it slip that we are a little desperate here. My apologies."

Debra laughed and waved at Andrew as she slid her chair out from the desk.

"We are desperate! Facts, Andrew! Facts. No apologies required. Ever. I don't know what I would do without you. I love you, Andrew. This is wonderful news. Yes, of course, I will interview him now. Let's go meet, Mr. Alan McClain."

Debra stood up; she walked over to the doorway and met Andrew.

The old front desk clerk reached over, hugged Debra Winston, and whispered, "I love you, too. Mrs. Winston . . . you are my family. I only wish hope, joy, and peace for you. Maybe this man, this Mr. McClain, is the answer to so many things. Our prayers and our hope to get some help here and keep the dream of the inn alive. I mean, it is Christmas. A magical time!"

"Magic, Andrew. Magic at Christmastime. We sure need a great, big dose of some magic right now."

"Exactly, and to have faith and always believe, Mrs. Winston. Always believe."

Alan McClain looked up when he saw Andrew return to the front desk and then he stood up when the woman approached him. My goodness, she was so young and very beautiful. Stunning! She was of medium height, neatly kept shoulder-length brown hair that she parted in the center of her head, with one side wave of her hair neatly tucked behind her left ear, and she had perfect facial structure with high cheekbones and wide doe-like brown eyes. As beautiful as her eyes were, and Alan noted that they were indeed very beautiful, she wore some sadness around those same eyes. She seemed exhausted, and her wide eyes allowed a glimpse of her soul to work through them. Her perfect figure fit very nicely inside a wool brown sweater and she wore a pair of tightly fitting black jeans that hugged her curves rather nicely. She topped it all off with leather boots pulled up just north of the top of her mid-ankles. The boots had a set of silver buckles on the side and they made a gently jingling noise while she walked and as her steps struck the floor of the lobby. The buckles signaled the gentle approach of the gorgeous woman.

Alan expected a much older woman. Perhaps, because of Andrew Gleason's age or just because of a ruthless or incorrect stereotype, Alan expected the owner to look much different than she did. On their telephone call, Jack told him that she was a widow. Lost her husband and it was a sad situation. Alan could see the picture clearly right now. How could one woman own and operate all of this business on her own? It was daunting, to say the least. She must be a quite remarkable and strong woman.

While she approached, Alan's eyes darted around her and he tried not to focus upon her glorious beauty or her magnificent parts and pieces, but he did make a careful note of the fact that she still wore her wedding ring on her finger.

Powerful grief. Holding on to her love for as long as she could do so.

He felt his own ring finger and the groove in his skin from where his wedding ring once sat. He pawned the ring last Wednesday. He did not want any reminders of his pain. This was a new start. A chance at a new life. He could feel it.

'Wow!' Debra Winston thought as she approached the man standing up next to the fireplace holding the job application in his hand. 'He is extraordinarily handsome. Tall, big hands and long fingers, a great build even tucked and hidden into that heavy winter vest, fantastic hair and woah . . . sexy stubble on his face. My goodness. I want him to stand there for a few more minutes and then turn around for me.' Debra Winston tried to hide her admiration of Mr. Alan McClain, but it was not easy to do so. For the first time since her husband passed, she felt a strong hint of attraction and a powerful ache in her loins. It had been a while since she felt the warmth and love of a man. As much as she loved him and he was very handsome; Andrew did not count!

"Hello, Mr. McClain," Debra said as she recovered from his good looks, she swallowed, and spit out the words, "Thank you so much for your interest in the open position and for coming in. I am, Debra Winston."

For some reason, she left off the honorific. No, not for some reason. She left it off on purpose. Whom was Debra kidding? Debra extended her hand out to Alan. He gently grasped it, and in an instant, Debra felt his warmth. She smiled, and he smiled too, and his eyes glowed and she took a deep breath as she felt his gentle power. Right then and there, Debra knew that she would hire him.

"Thank you, ah, ah, Mrs. Winston." Alan had noted that

Andrew Gleason had referred to her as Mrs. Winston, but she left off the title when they met. Alan made keen note of such things and decided to go the neutral route. "Ah, ah, yes. Here is my application," Alan stammered as he studied her eyes. She was so gorgeous, and he felt an instant attraction to her that he needed to shake off rather quickly. This potentially could be his boss. Nevertheless, she was stunning. When his eyes wandered around the interior of the lobby, then he glanced at the glorious Christmas tree and then to the snow falling outside just beyond the glow of the window Christmas lights; Alan already felt as if he found Christmas magic.

Debra took the application from Alan and she waved in the direction of the guest chair in front of the fireplace. "Please call me, Debra. Please sit down and relax, Mr. McClain. . .."

Alan cut her words off gently.

"Alan. Please call me, Alan. Is that okay, Debra?"

He immediately sat down after speaking, and Debra greatly admired his forthrightness. A Jersey guy. No doubt. His accent was a growl and rather sexy, too. Debra sat opposite him and Andrew suddenly appeared, asking if they wanted any coffee or tea, or water. He was the perfect host. Alan thanked Andrew and shook his head to indicate no and Debra asked for a cup of coffee and thanked Andrew. After Andrew hustled off to obtain the coffee, Debra opened the job application and studied it carefully. Alan studied her eyes as they traveled across the lines, words, and pages. He was a little anxious, as she remained silent. Finally, after Andrew delivered the coffee, a party of guests arrived in the lobby for check-in, and what seemed as if it was eternity passed between them; Debra spoke and finally answered his question.

"That is fine. Yes. Please call me, Debra. In studying

your application here, all I can say is, my goodness, Alan. You do have wonderful and diverse experience. Almost twelve years at the Farber Dye Factory down there in Haledon. In charge of repairing, maintaining, and operating most . . . everything. Why did you leave? Andrew told me the story of coming in here looking for direction to Jack Kemp's place. He is a military friend of yours. I know Jack. He is a hard worker and a quality man. Runs a popular restaurant, too. Successful. You were going to help Jack out and fix some things for him and stay over for the Christmas holidays. It is a very interesting story of how you drove in here, in the heart of Sussex County, in a snowstorm, saw our sign, chatted it up with Andrew, and now, you are applying for this job. Why would a man of your vast experience not want to find a job in a larger facility? A facility that would pay you more, and perhaps provide more in the way of benefits and such things as pension plans and other perks for you."

Mrs. Debra Winston asked all the correct questions and Alan knew that this was woman was a sharp, top-notch businessperson, who was not only beautiful, but she was incredibly smart, too.

"Well, I left for a few reasons. One, to be factual and not to give out too much personal information but to be factual, my wife left me for a wealthy executive that she fell in love with at her job who could buy her what she wanted in life and a poor maintenance man could not. I am now recently divorced. My ex-wife is happy, and I guess that to me, is what matters the most."

Alan took a deep breath and his eyes wandered around the lobby and it seemed as if they settled on the Christmas tree and the fantastic lights glowing there in front of them. He gathered strength from the joy and continued to explain.

"I have pain from it all, but no ill wills or feelings. My best wish is that I wish her happiness. I left because I was tired of breathing in nasty dyes and chemicals and other horrible stuff and most of all—I left to leave everything behind and to begin a new life. Looking around here, I can feel the joy. The challenge. It feels as if this amazing facility needs me. Needs a loving caretaker. Sure, money is important, but so is your spirit. Your purpose. Your mission in life. I am a military man—I thrive with missions."

Debra blinked a few times before answering. Yes, she thought, this was a factual and forthright man. Honest and trustworthy. And she tried to remove the thoughts from her mind, but it was futile. Alan McClain was very sexy, and handsome, too. A man who had skills, with many trades, and who was a hardworking man. Not some stuffy, useless executive. A man's man. They are very hard to find nowadays. And he was single. Her mind wandered in a thousand directions. Perhaps a million directions would be more factual.

Debra said, "I appreciate and respect your honesty and forthrightness. Thank you for sharing what brought you here. I am sure that was a difficult situation."

Debra Winston waved her hands in the air and then she folded them in her lap. It seemed as if she was trying hard to ensure that she had all the details of Alan's situation.

"So, let me understand all of this. You left this job, your life in Paterson and Haledon behind, you jumped in your car, to visit and help your friend and to clear your mind and enjoy the holidays and found yourself in Sussex County in the midst of snowstorm, got lost, and saw our sign and here you are?" Debra asked and she took a sip of her coffee and peered at Alan over the rim of her coffee cup.

The guests completed the check in process at the front desk and made their way to the elevator. Andrew leaned in to eavesdrop without being too obvious. He failed because he was way too obvious.

Alan answered right away, "Yes. Correct. Hey, it is Christmastime. Christmas magic is all around us all. I had originally thought that I would head to Newark, or Jersey City, or maybe central Jersey or to the shore. However, when I spoke to Jack and he invited me up here, said I could help him out and we could hang out like in the old days, it seemed very cool. Calming. This atmosphere is awesome. The ski resort, this quaint downtown area. So, here I am. I love the cold, the snow, pine trees and fresh air. Anything but chemicals and cities. Therefore, in retrospect, I guess in my own mind that I crossed off Newark and Jersey City! I guess that I needed the country even though I am a city kid."

Alan leaned in and smiled. He waved his hands in the air to encompass the lobby of the Vernon Valley Inn.

"Hey! Wow! Look at this wonderful lobby! It is fantastic. I love buildings. That is what I do. I take care of buildings and this one is very special. The Christmas tree, the fireplace, the colors of the lights, the greens on the railings. It is all about Christmas and joy! I truly need Christmas this year and I badly need some joy. You need help and a top-notch maintenance person. Here I am. A win-win. In my opinion, at least."

He felt some confidence and went for the brass ring.

"Please. Debra, you can call my foreman there on the application. He will vouch for me. He tried to give me a big raise to make me stay on, but it was not about the dough. It was about my life. My mental and physical health. My future. A job is a job, but life is about so much more than just a job. Ya gotta feel it, be happy, and take something from both your life and your work. The military taught me to be factual, the city taught me to be tough, and I have skills that you need. You can speak to Jack, too. You know he is a stand-up guy."

Alan stopped speaking, and he made eye contact with Debra. Her heart skipped a few beats, and so did Alan's heart! It was an instant and powerful attraction. Alan needed to continue to speak his thoughts to break the stare, or otherwise, he might fall in love with his potential new boss. Right then and there. Or perhaps he already had done so.

Alan took a deep breath, allowed his eyes to wander off Debra's beautiful face and over to the front desk lobby where Andrew stood.

"Andrew there, he said you were desperate and I don't know the entire picture. But I can tell you that I need this job and as I said, you need my skills and experience and this building and property needs me. I can feel it. I can fix anything and if you hire me and show me where that snowplow is, then I will clear that lot of snow and work my butt off to make this the best holiday ever for you, for me, for Andrew, for your business, and mostly for the guests."

Debra shook off her careful study of Alan's remarkable facial features and the sexiness of his Jersey accent, which was more of a husky growl. She tried to push aside the powerful attractions. As best she could do so.

Debra smiled and said, "Well, Alan, you are very convincing and, of course, you are correct . . . it is all about our guests."

Right on time, at the speaking of those words, more Christmas magic intervened as a large group of guests arrived. They shook off the snow on their boots and they promptly headed for the front desk to check in.

Alan and Debra both stopped speaking when they overheard one of the guests commenting to Andrew that they hoped that the maintenance crew would properly plow the parking lot so they could get out and head for the ski resort without any issues. Their car had some difficulty making the gentle grade into the parking lot from the main road. Andrew looked over at Alan and Debra and then turned his attention to the guests. He assured them that it would be in good condition. Shortly.

Debra knew what to do. She needed to act fast. Right now, to hire Mr. Alan Francis McClain. She did not need to call any references or check into any of his background. The connection was firm; it was strong, and it was powerful. All of this felt as if it was how it was supposed to be.

"You indicated that you can start right now. What about your pay? I see here on your application the wage figure that you earned there at the factory and that is a very good wage. I am not sure that I can match that right now. . .."

Alan jumped into the conversation again and cut off Debra's words.

"Pardon the interruption. Respectfully, please, I understand. As I said. It is not about money. I will take whatever pay you feel is fair. I have all my tools packed in my car. I have all my life and all my clothes in that vehicle, and, yes, I will start right now. Show me the keys to the snowplow, show me the maintenance shop, show me the snow blower and hand me the snow shovel. Please give me the work orders and I will take care of them all. I do need to bump out to see Jack and help him with what he needed. A promise is a promise to a friend. I will take care of everything here first." Alan swallowed hard and pondered the next statement, but he knew he needed to stick to the facts. He explained, "I was going to stay with Jack in his spare room while I was here. I do need a room to stay in until I find a place of my own in these parts, but you can call those landscapers and those contractors and tell them to cancel any work here. Save the big bucks, they are gonna try to charge you. You just say the word, Debra and Mr. Alan Francis McClain has you covered."

Behind the front desk of the Vernon Valley Inn, Mr. Andrew Gleason burst into spontaneous applause. After realizing the fact that not only did Alan and Debra know that he was eavesdropping on their conversation, but that he had interrupted a business meeting, Andrew stopped applauding, and he mumbled an apology. The front desk clerk then picked up some papers on the front desk and fiddled around with them in order to create a diversion. Alan laughed and so did, Debra, as she stood up and bowed and waved in Andrew's direction.

"I am so glad you approve, Andrew, and . . . so do I. Welcome to the Vernon Valley Inn, Mr. Alan Francis McClain, chief engineer, and snow removal expert. A room is not any trouble. Andrew will book one for you. We still have a few left open. We can work out the details. Please, do go and grab your tools, let me change into my winter boots, grab my winter coat and hat and I will show you where that snowplow and where the maintenance shop and the tools are located. It will give us great pleasure to call off those contractors. We need to do some human resources related paperwork. I will get that and you can fill it out. . .."

Alan gently grabbed her arm and she felt a chill up her spine at his grip.

Alan was very excited and his voice reflected the excitement.

"Great! Thank you so much! I am ready to go. Right now! Please, Debra. Time is important here. That snow is piling up out there. Can we do that paperwork later? I want to get out there right now."

Debra smiled at his willingness.

"Yes. you are correct. We can do that later. Let's go. Now."

Alan stood up and pointed at Debra's boots and commented, "I kinda like those, but I guess they are not so good in the snow."

His words warmed her heart.

Debra smiled widely and lifted her left foot in the air while balancing her weight on her right foot. "Thank you. Yes, they are my favorite boots but yes, you are correct. They are not so good in the snow. . .."

Alan fell in love. Perhaps for the second time today. Love at first sight, times two. This time it was with the maintenance shop. His new domain.

"Wow! Great maintenance shop and garage. This snowplow truck is old, but it looks solid."

Debra watched as Alan scanned his new shop and the tools and surroundings. He had set an enormous tool box down next to one of the workbenches. Debra wondered how he hauled it from his car all the way into the shop without using a hand truck. It looked as if it weighed a ton or more. Alan was very strong. No question.

Mr. Alan Francis McClain jumped into the old snowplow and turned the ignition key. Of course, it did not start. Debra's heart sunk.

Her face reflected her disappointment.

She said, "Oh my. My fault. I should have run the engine occasionally and kept the battery up to snuff. I just have so many other things to do." Alan was already out of the truck and scanning the tools and equipment. He spotted what he needed and plucked it out of the maze of tools and equipment.

"I gotcha. Not a problem. This is what you pay me for. I am on it. This battery charger will do the trick. I will have this rolling in no time. While the battery charges, please show me the snow blower and snow shovel. I can start clearing snow off the sidewalks and curb cuts."

Debra did so and, in short order, Alan was blowing the snow off the sidewalks and shoveling as if he was a snow machine working on blowing the snow up on the nearby ski slopes. Debra stood and watched him work and then she realized that she was not just supervising a new employee to make sure he was doing the job, she was admiring him. He was so handsome. Rugged, and he seemed tireless and impervious to the cold. How and why would his wife leave him for another man? He seemed as if he was a godsend. Just in time.

Debra broke her gaze and thoughts; she realized that she was idle and wasting time. She grabbed a snow shovel and walked down the sidewalk to help Alan clear the snow off the last section. Alan stopped his work when he saw Debra working behind him on the walkways.

"What'cha doing, boss?" He asked.

Debra stopped shoveling. She looked up and had a puzzled look on her face. She pushed her wool hat back on her head and answered.

"Ah, I am helping you?"

Alan shook his head and said, "Nah, nah, nah. You are the boss. I got this. You need to go inside, get warm and take care of boss things. I appreciate the gesture, but this is what you pay me for."

He smiled and walked over and gently reached for the snow shovel and took it from her. She handed it off easily.

"Sorry. You are correct. Old habits don't go away easily. I guess that I grew accustomed to doing everything myself. Thank you."

"No, Debra. Thank you."

His smile melted any snow out of her heart and warmed

her soul. Alan thought she was the loveliest snow bunny that he ever saw. All bundled up in a winter coat, that despite the thickness of the material, it still hugged her curves and displayed her perfect female figure, the wool hat on her head, her beautiful eyes, her smile. The joy of her facial expression in realizing that he was here now and there was hope. Hope for the both of them. Everything was going to be all right.

Debra Winston smiled and said, "Well. I will go inside and do boss things. See you in a bit. Come inside for a break and cup of coffee whenever you want."

"I will. Thank you," Alan said as he went back to work. "Once I finish my job."

Debra waved and walked away. Alan might have admired the rear view of her as she left. My goodness, she was gorgeous. When Debra walked into the lobby of the inn, she wore a mile-wide smile. Good old Andrew. He had spent a lifetime of reading people's body language. He knew. Andrew knew.

Christmas magic.

The old desk clerk rushed from behind the front desk and all he did was rush over to Debra. He gave her a warm and powerful hug. A fatherly hug. She knew that Andrew knew.

It was that old Christmas magic with a touch of love at first sight mixed in

Everything was going to be all right and Mr. Alan Francis McClain was here to stay.

For a very long time.

A few hours later and the inn was now nearly at full

occupancy.

The snowfall was easing, but still steady. Debra finally had a break from assisting Andrew with check-ins and front desk work. She looked up when she heard the rumble of the snowplow truck and the scraping of the blade on the parking lot surfaces.

Debra asked her faithful employee, "Oh my, Andrew. Has Alan even come in for a break? Or a cup of coffee? He has been out there for hours and hours now."

"Not that I have seen. I will go and pour him a cup. I made a fresh pot only a few minutes ago. And he needs to take a walkie-talkie so we can contact him," Andrew said while he plucked a 2-way radio from the row of chargers, behind his position at the front desk, he smiled, and handed it off to Debra. She took it and slipped it into her pants pocket.

"Besides, it will give you an excuse to spend time with Alan and talk to him some more." Andrew said with a wink. Debra blushed.

She smiled and mumbled, "Okay. I will get my coat and hat. Yes. Please pour a cup of coffee and put a lid on it. Thank you!"

Alan spotted Debra waving her arms as she stood in front of the inn. He made a quick pass with his blade, then lifted it off the ground with the hydraulics and shifted gears and turned to meet her. She was holding a cup of coffee in her hand. Alan stopped in the front of the inn. He leaned over and opened the passenger side door of the truck.

"Climb in. Too cold out there. What'cha need, boss?"

Debra rather nimbly jumped up in the high truck and Alan made note of her flexibility and strength. Work was part of her life now. Hard work.

"Here you go, Alan. I brought you a cup of coffee. Thought you could use it. You have been out here forever. I thought you said you would come in. And I lost track of the time." She closed the door and settled into the seat as she handed off the hot coffee to Alan.

The grateful snowplow operator smiled and took the coffee. Alan gently poked the slot in the coffee cup lid open with his finger.

He said, "Yeah. I lost track, too. This is great. Thank you. Just have to make a few more passes and we are finished up here. Snow is easing now."

Debra smiled and reached for the seat belt and harness and buckled it up and then, with a pat of the dashboard, she said, "Okay. Cool. Well, let's go then. Hop to it. I have never been in a snowplow truck before. Please give me a snowplow lesson. Not that I could drive it. Have to practice my manual transmission and clutch stuff, but you can teach me. Someday. When I was seventeen, I had a powder blue stick-shift Sunbeam. I can do it. Just need practice."

Alan McClain took another sip of coffee, then placed it in the cup holder on the dashboard of the truck while stealing glances at his new boss. Indeed, Alan was in trouble now. For sure, he thought she was the cutest snow bunny and woman that he had ever seen. Christmas magic hit him, too. He shifted gears, lifted the clutch, dropped the plow blade, and eased into the roll.

"I have no doubt. Powder-blue Sunbeam, huh? That fits you. Okay, boss. Well, this old truck weighs a bit more. This dial controls the blade. Up and down and right and left. Like twiddling a radio knob. Here we go."

And they went around the parking lot and they talked and he explained the process. His skills mesmerized her. It was so much more difficult than she could ever imagine. There was an art and a skill to snow removal. After the lots were clear of snow, Alan explained how to spread salt from the tailgate spreader.

"This knob controls the speed of the throw and spread. Along with truck speed. You see it in the side view mirror there."

Debra peered in and nodded as Alan explained.

"The weather is a large part of my job. It directly affects my job duties and the requirements for how the facility operates. Each season brings new adventures and challenges in operating facilities and keeping everything up to snuff. Obviously, we have snow removal. Then heat and humidity with air conditioning. And spring with landscaping renewals and warmer temperatures and fall with leaves and cold arriving. I checked the weather for tonight. Going down to fifteen degrees. Still okay to spread salt. If it gets down to single digits, then salt is not effective. In fact, not only do you waste money by throwing it all around, you actually can make more ice."

Debra leaned back in the passenger seat and she smiled and sighed. She had not been this relaxed in forever. Since Before Gordon fell ill. Forever ago. Now, this glorious, handsome man suddenly arrives and everything changed in a single day. A moment in time. She felt the need to convey and explain some more to Alan. He made her so comfortable. Just like Gordon did.

"I can't thank you enough, Alan. My goodness, this day has been magical. Since Gordon, my husband, died in April of this year. It has been so difficult. This inn . . . it was his family business for a very long time. Their dream. After his parents passed, it became Gordon's dream. Then he became so sick and he passed so quickly. I felt as if I had to keep the business going for him. Then everything came crashing down."

Alan focused on the truck and his driving, but he

nodded and caught Debra out of the corner of his eye.

"I am so sorry. I can't imagine how difficult that was for you."

"It was unbelievable." Debra waved in the air with her hands to emphasize the point.

"First the long-time chief engineer had to retire and move away to take care of his elderly parents, then the restaurant owners and operators decided to retire and I have not been able to find suitable partners to reopen it. The restaurant is a huge part of this business. Guests want to have the convenience of meal and dining options attached to our lodging. I considered taking on the restaurant operations on my own, but it is too much for me. That business is so difficult, and I know nothing about it. The closing greatly affected our business, but we kept it going somehow. I had to do most everything myself or hire expensive contractors. I learned how to fix toilets. I can do some things but not great. It is so difficult to hire employees. Especially here in Sussex County. Most folks commute downstate to better-paying jobs. Andrew is amazing, but he is old now. He has been here forever. Still, I could only put so much on him. Andrew has helped me though this all. He is like a father to me. I have no other family left. Other than some cousins, neither did Gordon. We come from small families."

Suddenly, Debra felt the overwhelming need to become emotional. Very emotional. The tears came like a flood.

"Hey! Boss! C'mon. It is okay now."

Alan checked the rear-view mirror and then pushed the clutch in and shifted to neutral. He pulled up the parking brake and reached over to embrace Debra.

"C'mon, I have you. Please don't cry. We have this."

She fell into him like it was supposed to be. He felt her

warmth and inhaled her glorious scent. She did the same. He smelled like a combination of winter and man. She knew right then and there that in his arms was where she was supposed to be. He reached over and flicked her tears away and she looked up at him, with wide-open eyes and an open heart, too. There were a few seconds of closeness. Her lips were so inviting, and he felt the need to kiss her. She felt the need to kiss him. Employee or not. Knowing each other for only a few hours did not matter, either. She just knew that everything about this day, and about Alan, was perfect.

Timing is everything in life. The walkie-talkie in her pocket crackled with Andrew's voice.

"Come in Alan!"

Andrew was slightly frantic.

They broke the embrace, as Debra wiped her eyes of the tears, snapped back to reality, and she reached for the radio and exclaimed, "The walkie-talkie radio! I almost forgot about it. I brought it out to you. It is for communicating with staff. And for emergencies."

Alan sat back and said, "Sounds like we have one."

Andrew returned to the radio.

"We have a flood in room two hundred and thirty-four. The sink waterline broke! We cannot shut it off at the water valve. I tried. Oh my. Help!"

Alan motioned for the radio and Debra handed it off to him. Alan keyed it and said, "Hang on, Andrew. Bail until we get there! We finished with the snowplowing. I will grab my tools and be there in a flash! Hang on!"

Alan put the truck back in gear, lifted the parking brake off, and popped the clutch.

"I will head for the shop to grab my tools. Stay with me

and show me how to get there."

Debra nodded and said, "Alan, about my emotions. I am so sorry. It is not proper behavior for me to act this way in front of an employee. . .."

He cut her off.

"Boss. No sorry ever. I gotcha. I am here now. I knew from the second that I walked in the front lobby that this is the place that I am supposed to be. We have this. Together."

That was it. She was officially in love with this man. In just a few short hours. Within a few words. Remarkable but true.

Christmas magic.

"Alan, please call me, Debra. Never call me boss. Please."

His smile melted her heart.

It only took a few turns of his skilled hands with a few hand tools to shut down the flood. Luckily, in the shop stash of spare parts, Alan found a new shutoff valve and sink supply line, and the sink was back in operation. Thank goodness because the inn was officially full. If Alan did not repair the waterline, there were no other rooms to move these guests into. The only spare room was Alan's room!

Debra worked the wet-vacuum to clean up the water. Once more, luck smiled on them, as Andrew's efforts kept the water contained to the tile of the bathroom and the flood did not encroach on the carpeting in the main areas of the room. For their inconvenience, Debra offered the guests a free day on their hotel stay and all was well once again.

Debra realized that they had made a great team. It was easy to see; in fact, one of the family of the guests in the "flood room" commented on Alan and Debra's chemistry together. Debra blushed when the guest said, "How her husband worked so well with his wife."

Debra kindly explained the situation, and the fact that she was a widow, but still wore her wedding ring.

The guest, an older woman, smiled and patted her arm and said, "Oh, well, my apologies. I saw your wedding ring and assumed. Well, you are an exceptional team. He is very handsome and you are lovely. A man who can handle tools is very sexy, too. Life is a funny thing and it goes on and on. Regardless, with all things considered, that man is very special. I am old. I can tell."

Suddenly, it was six o'clock at night. Andrew left for his fill-in shift and a young college-age gal took over at the front desk. Alan realized that he never even ate lunch and it now was dinnertime. He had a bold suggestion. Yet, it was practical. The snowstorm ended. Everything was under control.

Alan felt exhausted, but fulfilled.

"Hey, Debra. I never got back to Jack. I think he closes at seven. What do you say, I call him up and we bump over there for dinner? Maybe a few beers? I am starving. Would you care to join me? Besides, I have an idea that I would like to present to my old army buddy." Debra smiled and tucked her hair behind her ear. She dressed in a sweatshirt, sneakers, and a pair of black dungarees that would set any man on fire with the hugs on her curves.

Debra's heart leaped at his words and the suggestion.

"Sure. Sounds great to me. I am starving, too. We never stopped all day. Idea? What kind of idea? Old Army ideas? Sounds dangerous."

"Nah. Sorry. Not going to let the cat out of the bag. It is a surprise. But if I know Jack, and man-oh-man, we chewed some of the same dirt together for a few years, he is going to love this idea."

"Okay. I am not going to get in between two old Amry buddies. You make the telephone call. Let me grab my coat and hat. Let's take the snowplow truck. I love riding in it!"

It was a glorious reunion of old military friends. A brotherhood; never broken. It was more than teamwork; it was courage, love, and support of a different kind. Willingness to die for one another and for a cause.

Debra sat at a table, sipping a cold beer, and admired the interaction. So genuine. So powerful. It was what she needed to see to confirm how special a man that Mr. Alan Francis McClain was. Yet, she already knew that was a fact. She knew the moment that he told her that he forgave his ex-wife and wished her only the best. Any man who could take that sort of pain was a strong and very special man. A man with a warm heart and forgiveness as an attribute. Forgiveness. She knew that forgiveness equals love. And she longed to be part of his love.

Jack Kemp closed his restaurant for the day. It had a been a long, but successful day. Business was excellent. He cooked up some cheeseburgers, some fries, and a side salad full of greens and goodies that would make one think it was June, rather than shortly before Christmas. They had more than just a few beers. They laughed, and shared military stories and adventures.

Debra sat and relished all of it. It had been so long since she enjoyed a social night out. To share in laughter and joy and to relax.

The meal was simple but it was glorious—exceptional.

When Jack mentioned how busy it was today and how

he had to turn away so many potential patrons because his place was so small, the ski resort was hopping, and his establishment had gained such a reputation for quality food, Alan struck at the moment. His idea. It was as if he was waiting on the sideline for just the right moment.

"I know a solution for that, Jack. I have just the right idea."

Jack looked over at his friend, took a sip of beer and titled his head to hear more.

"Oh yeah, Bud. What is on your mind?"

"The vacant restaurant attached to the Vernon Valley Inn. It is perfect for you. Now is the time to make the move. Expand. Make it happen. No more with The Hutch. It implies small. That is perfect for this joint but not for a bigger joint. I can get in there tomorrow and check everything out. I bet it is a turn-key facility with some minor work."

Alan waved his hands in the air as if to display a name. Debra and Jack followed his hands as they did so.

"Jack's Place. I bet you can transfer the liquor, beer, and wine license over and open in no time at all. Just in time for peak winter season. It will be a gold mine. Your smarts. Your food. The location. The vibe."

Jack's eyes lifted and Debra leaned forward in her chair.

Jack tilted his beer over and finished it off. You could tell that Alan hit home with his idea. He hit hard. Jack already knew that his current place was too small and his business and following had outgrown the size of the facility.

Jack Kemp said, "Well, Bud. I cannot argue with you. You have a great idea. The Chamber of Commerce representative came by here a few weeks ago and mentioned that the restaurant was vacant and he asked if I had any interest. I was really busy that day, as it has been lately. Which, of course, is a blessing. Honestly, I saw the signs and have thought about it before but just been too busy to pursue it. It is a huge step for me."

Alan knew his old friend very well. He jumped into the conversation at just the proper moment. He had a knack for doing that.

"Ah, yeah, Jack. This seems to be a no-brainer, my friend. Always busy. Turning patrons away because of a lack of space. Long waiting lines. Only a few tables. A small bar with only a few stools. Lost business because you outgrew your space. Seems to me that we have a solution. Right down the road from here."

Jack thought about how Alan was correct.

"And you will be around to do the repairs and maintenance?" Jack Kemp asked.

"Of course. We will be a team. Again."

Jack stood up, and he looked over at Debra and then at Alan.

Jack said, "I will get us some more beers."

He turned to head to the cooler to get another round of beers, then he quickly turned back and looked at Debra.

"I love the idea. I really do. My only apprehension is that I am not sure I can afford the rent, Debra. That is a big place. Huge bar. I will have to hire bartenders and servers, and you know how the labor market goes around here. Lots of dough. Big nut to crack."

Debra Winston was all in. She followed Alan's lead. She knew where this was heading.

"Name the rent. Whatever you think it should be and you can afford. It is yours. Having a thriving restaurant next to the inn is vital to my operation. In my college days, I had a part-time job tending bar. I will tend bar for you when I can break away from the business of the inn. I don't look too bad. Maybe I can jump in at happy hour and I will bring in customers. Jack, we can do this. Customers will come and all of us we will figure it out together."

Debra waved her hand in the air to fully encompass Alan, Jack, and herself.

"All of us. I see teamwork here and an amazing bond of brotherhood from the military. We will make it work."

Jack smiled and shook his head.

Jack said, "Okay. Wow! Very fair. I should have jumped at the chance a few months ago! I saw the for lease sign a hundred times and until now . . . until today, with the snow, and Alan here, and all of this business. . .."

"Magic. Christmas magic, Jack. That is the difference," Alan offered up. "You said it yourself. To me. Earlier today. On the telephone."

"I did. I sure did. Okay. Deal." Jack rushed over and he grabbed Debra's hand and he shook it fervently.

"Deal," Debra answered. "Please come by my office when you can and we can work out the details and draw up some papers with the realtor."

Jack pointed a thumb in the direction of Alan and added, "Okay. Will do. But this guy goes along with it."

Debra looked over at Alan and she answered without hesitation.

"That is the one thing non-negotiable. Alan is here to stay."

There were many hidden meanings in that statement. Jack sensed it.

Alan smiled and looked over at Debra and went out on a limb with his words.

"Besides, happy hour with Debra behind the bar will be a gold-mine. She does not just look good, she is gorgeous!"

Jack nodded. Alan continued to smile and Debra blushed as she tucked some strands of hair behind her ear.

Jack saw Debra blush, and he sensed the connection between his friend and Debra Winston. He moved quickly as to continue the mood of joy with a celebration suggestion. There was much to celebrate here!

"Forget the beers. I will pour us some shots to celebrate."

That night in her room, Debra Winston lovingly removed her wedding ring, and she kissed it. She fell to her knees and prayed. Then she wept. She wept for Gordon's love. For all they shared. Yet, she knew that it was time to move on and at the same time to glorify their love. She carefully tucked the ring away in her jewelry box. Along with heartfelt memories of love and times.

It was Christmas Eve. The time before, during and after, the holidays zip by like no other time of the year.

It was around four in the afternoon and it had been a sunny, but cold, and then a cloudy day. The sunset over Hamburg Mountain, mixed with glorious colors of mixtures of purple and red and a touch of yellow. Glorious. A Christmas Eve sunset.

The ski resort was operating at full tilt. I seemed as if you could hear the hum of the lifts and the swish of the skiers on the slopes from the Vernon Valley Inn. The peal of the church bells from the numerous small churches out on Route 23 echoed throughout the valley. Welcoming the worshipers the faithful. For unto us is born a savior.

Christmas Eve and the peace settled into the valley. A night like no other night.

Debra Winston went out on a mission to find Mr. Alan Francis McClain. He was always working on something. The man's energy was boundless. She could have used the radio; however, that would not be as much fun as tracking him down would be. He was not in the maintenance shop; nor was he in the garage. She spotted a light on in the restaurant. In Jack's Place.

'There he is,' Debra thought as she turned in that direction.

Opening day would be New Year's Eve. That was going to be an amazing day. For sure.

"There you are," Debra said, as she opened the side door of the restaurant and she found Alan behind the bar, tinkering with a plumbing supply line, feeding the beer taps. "Tinkering. It is Christmas Eve, Alan. Four o'clock. Time to quit for the day." Debra took a seat at the bar and she admired this glorious man. Her eyes reflected her joy and her love.

He looked up and smiled that killer smile. He placed his wrench on the bar.

"Done. All hooked up. Time to test them. You want the first pour?"

Alan asked as he grabbed a nearby beer glass and held it under the beer tap.

He continued to explain, "Have to test it. Jack had the kegs delivered today. Opening day looms. I have lots of things that I need to tinker with yet."

"Sure, pour me one. And you, too. You need to tinker, huh?" Debra asked rather seductively and suggestively.

Alan thought, 'Oh my. Debra has turned up the

romantic vibe. This is Christmas Eve. Magical in so many ways.'

He nodded and poured the beer. It spit a bit of air, but then the glorious beer flowed smoothly. He then grabbed another glass and poured himself a glass of beer, too. Yet Alan had a plan. Time to make a move. He could feel the mood. The vibe. Christmas Eve. A night of profound love.

Christmas magic.

"I will need to reserve some time to teach you a few things. One of them is how to drive that snowplow truck and give you a refresher on operating a manual transmission. That powder-blue Sunbeam was a little different from what the plow truck is. Might take me some time to show you all the proper moves."

Debra leaned forward on the bar and she never looked more gorgeous than she did right now. The downlights over the bar counter reflected her beauty. She sensed the mood now.

With a low growl to her voice, Debra said, "Show me some proper moves, huh? Tinker, huh? Okay, well, I am all in. What else do you have in mind other than working that old truck?"

He delivered the beer and made his move.

"I have a few ideas in mind. Let's start with this. First pour from Jack's place and a first kiss for us."

Alan leaned in and Debra dove in. Without hesitation. She never felt a kiss like that kiss. She moaned and embraced the back of Alan's head and rose into the passion.

Alan did too. Falling in love at Christmastime.

When they broke the kiss, they touched heads and Alan said, "That was better than I ever imagined."

Debra was breathless and wordless.

Alan walked over and grabbed his beer and carried it over to where Debra sat at the bar.

"To cover the beers, I will put a few dollars in the till for Jack. Merry Christmas Eve."

They toasted glasses and kissed again.

Debra whispered in his mouth.

"Merry Christmas Eve, Alan. Speaking of tinkering. I certainly have a few other things that you could tinker with, Mr. Alan Francis McClain."

Christmas magic.

The next day, Alan got down on his knees and unveiled a ring. . ..

Christmas magic.

Christmas Day of 1979 was very special. Alan Francis McClain Junior had a truckload of toys underneath a fantastic Christmas tree. Considering that he was just an infant; someday, soon, he would be able to play with them. Right for now, it was simply a display of love.

His proud and overzealous father might have miscalculated his exact age.

The toolbox was a giveaway.

Mrs. Alan Francis McClain smiled at her husband's overzealousness. Debra could not have been prouder. It was just over a year ago when he arrived in her life. To save her; to love her; for her to save him; for her to love him.

That was a remarkable day, when Alan wandered into their inn; lost, but somehow found at the same time.

Snow fell outside. Inside, it was warm, and it was peaceful.

The locals that lived here forever and a little bit more, always said when the wind blows out of the north, from High Point to Butler, across Hamburg Mountain and it whistles down from the point, then change is on the way. If the wind whistles just before Christmas arrives; then it brings with it a gentle and extra special touch of magic.

It appears as if the local folks were correct.

THE END

13

Flash!

The Sunday that the Bell Fell

The Worsley family had overseen the ringing of the church bell for as long as most of the parishioners of the little church recalled. At the Call to Worship and after the Recessional and the Benediction, one of the family members, rang the church bell in the tower. Ten tugs on the rope that wound its way from the bell tower to behind the Altar.

Ring that bell; proclaim God's glory for a mile or so. Give or take, depending upon how clear the air was, to carry the sound through the noise of the world.

The family alternated the bell-ringers on a rotational basis through the family members. First, it was Chuck, then Shawn, then Nadia, and then Sharon. If it was a special holiday service, then often, they all would ring the bell together. No one was sure how it began with the Worsley family taking the role of the official bell-ringers for the church, but the tradition continued forever.

It was a small church; a heavy oak wood interior full of dark finishes. Glorious stained-glass windows lined each side of the sanctuary. The Altar area had a Lectern and a Pulpit, and the Pastor Bench, and the choir sat behind them in rows of robed musical aspirations. An education building attached to the sanctuary at a right angle, and the basement had a fellowship hall and a small kitchen.

All under the control of God's glory.

Pastor Lumpkin had been the pastor at the church for over twenty years. He was quite short and diminutive in stature. In fact, he used a box behind the Pulpit to lift himself up the microphone. Everyone knew the good pastor for his kindness; Hellfire and Brimstone were not in his sermon mixtures. However, he tended to be a bit long-winded in the Pulpit. Not boring, that would be too harsh for Christians to say to describe Pastor Lumpkin's sermons. Long-winded was a kinder term.

He seemed to be especially long-winded when there was a big sporting event on television and radio at one in the afternoon.

The young father sat in the first pew on the left side of the sanctuary. Often, his little son sat next to him. The boy was well-behaved for a three-year-old. The young father oversaw audio taping the worship services for the shut-ins of the congregation. Sitting where he did, allowed him access to a side door, which led to a room where they kept the audio recording equipment contained. The young father often had to tend to the tapes and equipment; therefore, worshippers grew accustomed to him getting up and down during the service. He did so silently and gracefully. Even while towing his son along, too.

One Sunday in spring, right after Easter. . ..

The Yankees played the Red Sox at one in the afternoon. It was an early season match-up of rivals.

Pastor Lumpkin was grasping at sermon straws to find the enthralling words to fit the time when Easter was over and Satan defeated. The sermon rambled on and on, like a freight train at a railroad crossing when you must use the bathroom. Occasionally, in the long string of cars, a freight car passes by that is colorful or has some interesting graffiti on it or some inventive painted obscenities; however, most of the experience is bores-ville.

The Yankees fans in the congregation kept checking their watches. And one Red Sox fan, too.

And Mrs. Tudley, who had a Sunday roast in the oven.

Just when Pastor Lumpkin was running out of Acts of the Apostles, he pulled the ultimate sermon straw out of the pack. For some reason, lost to time, Pastor Lumpkin for special effects, or to wake the congregation up, or a combination thereof, he had prearranged for Nadia Worsley to ring the tower bell at a specific time.

The good pastor gave a gentle nod in the direction of Nadi and she rose up out of the pew and gave a nod in return. The parishioners, who were still awake, squirmed in their seats. The choir behind Pastor Lumpkin scooted their robed backsides to the edge of the seats; something different was occurring! Something of interest!

Pastor Lumpkin's usual monotone drone grew louder and his voice deepened. Since he was a small man in stature, that was a monumental feat!

He tapped his fist (Pulpit pounding was not in his repertoire) on the Pulpit and spoke out, "And because of the defeat of Satan, and the joy of our salvation, I say we proclaim of the joy of Christianity and ring our church steeple bell now as a testimony of joy!"

And with those words, in the hallway behind the Altar, Nadia gave a tug on the old rope leading to the bell in the tower.

"RING! RING! RING, AND A THUD!"

A thud?

A loud thud that shook the foundations of the church. Pastor Lumpkin stopped preaching. Everyone tilted an ear and looked around at each other.

Murmurs of curiosity broke out throughout the

Sanctuary.

"What was that?"

Then another sound rattled throughout the sanctuary.

A descending, "Bang!"

The Sanctuary shook. Everyone sat in pause. Wondering.

Another descending, "Bang!"

The Sanctuary shook. Everyone sat in pause. Wondering. Rinse repeat, but the noise grew closer, and louder, and the shaking was more intense.

Then came Nadia's scream! And she burst into the Sanctuary!

"The rope broke! The bell is falling!"

Oh, no! The bell tower loomed directly above the Altar and the choir pews!

Panic ensued, and the congregation began to stream out for the exits. The young father jumped into action. He was that sort of man. He grabbed his young son and then sprinted to the Altar as the bangs grew closer and closer!

The young father hustled the choir out of the choir pews all while Pastor Lumpkin stood frozen in the Pulpit. Once the choir was safe., the young father grabbed Pastor Lumpkin, all while still holding his son, and dragged him to safety.

Once clear of the Altar, the three of them dove for cover under the first rows of pews. The final bang resulted in the ceiling above the choir rows exploding, and pieces of wood, plaster, and ceiling materials splintered in all directions. Yet, due to the holy nature of the mission of the church, divine intervention occurred. Remarkably, the bell and its enormous weight crashed through the layers of ceiling, but before crashing into the choir loft and Altar area, it stuck onto a rafter that held it firmly in its hands.

Edges of brass stuck out of the ceiling. . ..

Through the dust and mayhem, while still sprawled out on the sanctuary floor, Pastor Lumpkin looked at the young father and his son and smiled and said, "Now, that was a sermon! Knocked that old church bell right out of the tower!"

The next Sunday, for the first time in forever, a member of the Worsley family did not tug on the rope to ring the bell.

Repairs to the beloved church bell were underway.

Instead, a tape-recording of a bell ringing played.

Chuck Worsley pushed the button.

14

Flash!

Winter into Spring

He always loved the winter.

Even as a little boy. Winter made him feel alive.

The cold, the wind, the ice, and the snow. Hockey on the frozen ponds. Christmas and the joy of the holidays.

His mother used to tell him, "Even as a little boy, in the summer, you would moan and groan and lay all around on the floor in front of a fan. I could not get you to go play outside. In the winter, you were gone and I could not find you until supper."

It invoked sadness in him when the seasons changed from winter into spring. He first felt the sadness when the signs slowly appeared that winter was leaving; such as when the snow melted and the robins returned. When the joy of Christmas was a forgotten memory and the sound of snowplows scraping the main street in front of his home and the chains on the snow tires of the city bus as it chugged on its route faded away. The sound that the winter wind makes in the snow-covered pines as it whipped through a snowstorm, swaying the branches and shaking loose snowy accumulations. The eerie silence of a snowy night when the stillness of the white peace settled in throughout the land.

When those winter sounds turned to the sounds of baseballs cracking off wooden bats and the pop of a fastball in a leather catcher's mitt replaced them.

When the cold slowly left and warmth took its place. When the warmer sunlight told the crocus and the snowdrops to try to poke their heads through the snow. He would miss when you worked or played outside in the snow all day, that exhausted yet exhilarated feeling that you get when you finally come inside and warm up. For him, it was unlike any other feeling. Satisfying. Hearty. Empowering. Sleeping under a warm blanket after a day outside in the cold and snow was the definition of heavenly sleep.

Yes, indeed, he always loved the winter. Now, he was old. He didn't feel that old, but some days, his back told him that he was. Sledding down the plowed hills of snow in the vacant lot next to his boyhood home on a bitterly cold January night might be out of the question now. However, if he could do so, he would still give it a try. When did he become sixty-six years old? It seemed as if he was just fifty! The last ten years were a blur. And now, here he was, once more.

The change of winter into spring.

Most of his life was now in the past. Yet, he vowed to keep moving. Keep working. Smiling. Too many people he knew retired and then died too young. He kept his purpose.

The man sat on the front stoop of his home. It was only a few days until Saint Patrick's Day.

It was cold last night, but now, at just past two in the afternoon, it was warm. The sun was warm on his face. The breeze was gentle. Most of the patches of the remaining snow were melting.

He enjoyed a cigar and a glass of Irish whiskey while sitting on that front stoop.

As a young boy, he sat on his front stoop all the time

and observed and was content. Their family home was on a busy street and he enjoyed watching the traffic, the people, and life go by. You can learn a lot about the world by sitting on your front stoop. He certainly did. It was quiet here on this front stoop. No busy city life whizzing by; yet he reflected on many things.

This afternoon, his mind wandered to regrets and mistakes, and things he should have done differently. To people he loved, to loves that he lost. To words that he did not speak, and words that he should not have said. His life.

A bit of sadness crept into his soul. Another sip of the whiskey, and another puff on the cigar.

Right now, he knew that many people would trade places with him. He was not wealthy, nor was he poor. He had a warm bed, a roof over his head, food in his belly, a cigar, and some whiskey. His memories. A simple life, yet he was lucky.

He shook off the sadness, and he smiled. Right now, he was content to be where he was, and for that fact, he was very thankful. Even though spring now peeked around the corner and slowly crept into his days, he would smile and embrace it and make the most of it. Being content is a gift that not many people receive.

He always loved the winter. Even as a little boy. Winter made him feel alive. Here he was again, on his front stoop. As if he was still a young boy. Watching, observing, and still learning. He was alive, as his favorite of the seasons passed him by once more. As the world around him shifted and changed, and moved.

Winter into spring.

15

Flash!

An Interview with an Evil, Mad Scientist

The Young Reporter: (Handsome to perfection. Perfect black hair. Perfect choppers. Spray tan. Blue eyes.) "We are here today to speak with Doctor Looneytune, the world-famous evil, mad scientist. We hope to find out what he is currently working on and discover some insight into what makes evil, mad scientists do what they do. Doctor, thank you for joining us. We appreciate you taking this time to meet with us. We know how busy your life is."

Doctor Looneytune: (grey wiry hair, standing up on end as if four-thousand-one-hundred and sixty volts of electricity at a very low current charged him up. He had wild bug eyes, thick glasses. Middle age. Strange accent like he is from eastern Hudson County New Jersey, or Romania, or a mixture of both.) "You are welcome. I sure am busy these days. Working on ways to destroy the entire world is not easy work."

The Young Reporter: "Oh, my! I imagine not! And what led you to this point? Why do you want to destroy the world, Dr. Looneytune?"

Doctor Looneytune: "Well, first off, I want to destroy the world because I am an evil, mad scientist and that is what we do. I read my job description. I did not intend to do this when I found out that I was a super-genius. I wanted to do good. But the world tainted me. In school, at a young age, evil children wronged me and they teased and bullied me about my hair. I had a bad childhood.

When I was only four-years-old, that bum, Santa Claus, brought me a Purple Panda, instead of a Pink Panther. You know, all the usual stuff."

The Young Reporter: "I understand. Santa can be unreliable at times. It can be very traumatic. Especially the creeping down the chimney part."

Doctor Looneytune: "Exactly."

The Young Reporter: "How do you intend to destroy the world, Doctor Looneytune?"

Doctor Looneytune: "Oh, very easily. I will detonate my super-gluteus-maximus incineration bomb over the North Pole. Take out that unreliable bum, Santa Claus first, and then the rest of the world will fall into ashes. POOF!" (Snaps his fingers. While bulging his eyes even more than before.)

The Young Reporter: "I see. Yes, take out the cause of your pain first. And the rest of the world suffers your wrath, too. Typical evil, mad scientist behavior."

Doctor Looneytune: "Exactly."

The Young Reporter: "But won't you go POOF, too?"

Doctor Looneytune: "Oh no. I will be under my whiz-bang, super-deluxe protection dome. Unscathed."

The Young Reporter: "Good plan. Did you create that device, too?

Doctor Looneytune: "No way. Ordered that sucker on the giant internet shopping machine site. Hell-u-va good price on their special shopping day."

The Young Reporter: "I see. And that brings us to another question. What will you eat and drink if you blow up and destroy the entire world except for your laboratory?"

Doctor Looneytune: "I invented a nutrition pill, and I

stockpiled beer, potato chips, water chestnuts, and canned hams."

The Young Reporter: "Okay. All the essentials. How about funding? Where do you get your funding from for all this evil creation business and for your secret, hidden laboratory that is twenty miles under Paterson, New Jersey, and your supplies and equipment?"

Doctor Looneytune: "Oh, those ding-dongs in the government send me free funding from grants. They think that I am working on ways to save the spotted-seven-toed-blobberfish. That sucker has been extinct for ten-thousand years. The dopes did not pay attention when they read the document. Especially on page nine-thousand and twenty-two where I buried my evil intentions within the ten-thousand-page document, of which all but eleven pages are exact duplicates of the same words and paragraphs."

The Young Reporter: "Wow. Tricky, tricky. But that is what evil, mad scientists do! You sure got them good on that one!

Doctor Looneytune: "Exactly. They are all dopes, anyway. Just want to head out for cocktail hour and get free meals, spray tans, and free baseball tickets. Say, how did you know about my secret, hidden laboratory that is twenty miles under Paterson, New Jersey?

The Young Reporter: "Oh, everything is hidden underneath Paterson, New Jersey. Plus, the location is on that internet map app."

Doctor Looneytune: "Geez. I never thought of that."

The Young Reporter: "Another question. How do you not know that some double-oh-seven type of secret agent or Detective Lyle Odell won't watch this interview and foil your evil plan two seconds before detonation?"

Doctor Looneytune: "Simple. Because they are both

fictional characters, and they do not exist! Ha! Ha! Ha!" (Rubs hands together stereo-typically during evil cackle.)

The Young Reporter: "Well, technically, we are both fictional characters and do not exist either. This kooky author wrote this drivel and made us up."

Doctor Looneytune: (Looks puzzled and rubs his chin) "Well, you got me on that one, young reporter. But you know what they say, 'There is a lot of truth to fiction.'"

The Young Reporter: "You do have a point. Well, this sure has been fun and very informative, too. This concludes this interview. Right now, I will go on the internet and order one of those whiz-bang super-deluxe protection domes. I suggest the rest of the population of the world should do the same. It seems as all you did was boost the sales even more of the giant internet shopping machine, Doctor Looneytune. Thank you for your time and the shopping tip! I have tons of stock in that company."

Doctor Looneytune: "Oh no! Curses! Foiled again!" (Hand-wringing ensues.) "Did I do okay there? Was that statement and the hand wringing perfectly stereotypical behavior of evil, mad scientists?"

The Young Reporter: "Absolutely. Perfectly stereotypical."

16

Flash!

Sunday Night
Tomorrow is a School Day

Memories.

Mom looks out the back porch window of the old wooden door. Her two children are in the backyard. Playing in the snow. All day. Except for when they came inside for lunch. Built a snowman. Built a snow fort. Had a snowball fight with the kids down the street. Pushed their sleds around in the yard.

Frozen stiff. Noses red. Toes cold. Socks soaked even with boots on.

Mom proclaims loud and clear out the back door.

"Tomorrow is a school day! Time for dinner now! Come on in. Get those boots off on the back porch. Set them on the newspaper that I put out there. Mittens off, too. Hang your coats and snow pants down by the furnace in the cellar. Don't track mud and snow and ice on my kitchen floor. I just mopped it yesterday! Come inside, now! Warm up. Wash your hands! Supper is almost ready!"

One of her children is brave. The boy; he is the youngest and his sister whispered to him to try.

"Ah, Ma! Can't we stay out for fifteen more minutes?"

"No! In! School day tomorrow. The weekend is over. Don't make me get your father!"

Moaning and groaning, but compliance.

Dad shouts from somewhere in the house, "Shut the back door! You are letting all the heat out! The furnace just kicked on again!"

Washed up and ready for supper. Dad has a beer. Mom has a glass of red wine.

"What's for supper?" The daughter asks.

"Meat loaf, mashed potatoes and gravy with green beans."

Moaning and groaning.

Dad stares them down. The big evil eye stare. Dad points at the oven door after Mom removes the food.

It was just enough of a stare to negate having to say, "There are children starving in the world who would love to have this dinner!"

Dad says, "Please, leave the door open. Let the heat out to help heat up the house."

Mom says, "Enjoy your supper. It is just what you need to fill you up after playing outside in the cold all day. If you clean your plates, you can have some apple pie for dessert."

Despite the initial moaning and groaning, it was a delicious meal. The children ramble on excitedly about their adventures while playing in the snow. Mother and father enjoy their children's excitement. The times we cherish. Times gone, but never forgotten.

"Please, Joan. Get me another beer," Dad asks.

Some laughs. Some fun. Family time. Another glass of wine for Mom. One more beer for the father. Slices of pie are all around.

"Okay, clear your plates. Let's wash the dishes now," Mom says.

Dad heads for his easy chair.

"Then after supper you can take your baths. You can watch some television, but bedtime is at seven o'clock. Sharp. School day tomorrow!"

Moaning and groaning. The daughter speaks first.

"Ah, Mom. Can't I stay up and watch Bonanza with you and Dad? I am older. Almost a teenager! I should be able to stay up later."

"No. school day tomorrow. Start drying."

The son took his turn.

"Can I listen to the hockey game on my transistor radio behind my pillow?"

"No. It is a school day tomorrow. You can watch Lassie and Wild Kingdom and then go off to bed. Start drying."

The daughter made a wish aloud. Pie-in-the-sky as it was.

"Maybe they will close the school tomorrow because of the snow?"

Mom rebuts it rather quickly.

"School will be open. The roads are all plowed. Besides, you played all day in the snow. Why would you not be able to walk to school?"

Moaning and groaning ensues.

Bath time. Only one bathroom. First goes the son. Then goes the daughter, and soon, they are on the living room floor in front of the wooden console black and white television, watching the famous collie save the day once more.

Then they are watching Marlin tame elephants and wild rhinos after peering out from behind some trees and weeds.

Mom says, "Off to bed now! No reading magazines and no hockey games on the radio. We will be up to tuck you in." First Mom, then Dad. Kisses and goodnights all around.

The children wait and listen in the dark. As soon as they hear the guitar intro music, out comes a magazine and a flashlight and click "on" goes the hockey game on the radio.

Dad knew. It was time for Dad to get in the game.

He did not even have to go to their bedrooms and check. He cupped his hands and bellowed.

"Dorothy, off with the flashlight and away with the teenybopper magazine! Paulie, shut off that radio! Bedtime. School day, tomorrow!

Soft moaning and groaning ensue. Compliance.

Soon there are dreams of snow, and snowmen, and snow forts and sleds. And of snowball fights. And of love. And of meat loaf and mashed potatoes.

The times we cherish. Times gone, but never forgotten.

Memories.

Spark

Noise Versus Silence

"It is easy to create noise, but creating silence is an art."

Spark

Sigh of Relief

"When the now, very old and decrepit, Big Bad Wolf had to have oxygen tanks delivered to his home, the Three Little Pigs exhaled a huge sigh of relief and canceled the building contractor's appointment."

Spark

Immeasurable

"How do you know if something is immeasurable, unless you try to measure it?"

Spark

Upside Down?

Little Boy: "Hey, Dad. If I turn my peanut butter and jelly sandwich upside down, is it now a jelly and peanut butter sandwich?"

Dad: "Go ask your mother."

Flash Plus

A Quiz on a Random Fire-Breathing Dragon Appearance

On a hot summer night in July just 'round midnight, if a random Fire-Breathing Dragon shows up on your front lawn, at your house in New Jersey, you should:

A: Immediately run back in your house and check your homeowner's insurance policy for incineration coverage by random Fire-Breathing Dragons. Be sure to read the fine print because those insurance agents are tricky and most likely have an exemption for random Fire-Breathing Dragons that cause total incineration losses.

B: Pull out your smartphone and scroll your contacts for Beowulf's number. Give him a ring and find out his immediate availability. Remind him to bring Naegling, the dagger, Wiglaf, and tell ole Beo not to forget a shield.

C: Negotiate with the Dragon. This might be to your advantage. After all, he might be able to light that pesky gas grille on the patio that never wants to light. Or maybe the Dragon will just char-broil a batch of hamburgers and toast some marshmallows, and you and your family can enjoy a late-night snack. Or ask if the random Fire-Breathing Dragon can incinerate that pesky patch of poison ivy in the backyard that comes back every year, despite blasting it with a tanker truck load of weed killer.

D: Stop being so damn cheap and upgrade to a better quality of Scotch whiskey that does not cause hallucinatory behavior.

E: Point the Fire-breathing Dragon in the direction of your next-door neighbor's house. The neighbor who complains about your dog barking and that you play your music too loud.

D: Pull out that smartphone, pose for a selfie with the random Fire-Breathing Dragon and post it on the Zip-Zok social media site. That sucker will go viral! You might be ashes by the time it hits, but at least you go out in a blaze of glory. It is worth taking the chance of total incineration, just to get likes and to be a social media influencer.

E: Get out that smartphone again and call the Pentagon. They sure could use a random Fire-Breathing Dragon in their arsenal. Might come in very handy. . ..

F: Check for proper local laws, taxes, permits, and licenses required for random fictional characters breathing fire in residential neighborhoods. Especially, without a very difficult to obtain, Fire-Breathing Dragon permit. This is New Jersey and chances are the random Fire-Breathing Dragon has run afoul of the local laws. Nowadays there is a permit, tax, and license for everything.

G: All of the above, except for selection D. D is for ding-dongs.

17

Flash!

Heavenly Baseball

Pastor Guggenheim Whorneout, had been the Senior Pastor since The Lutheran Church of the Saints, was a small, corner church on a lonely country road. In a stroke of keen foresight to the future, and led by God, the church's charter members purchased adjacent acreage next to the church property from a dairy farmer who wanted to move to Boreseville, Nebraska and start his life over. The dairy farmer's wife said he was too boring, and she ran off with the manager of the local food store.

To start a new life.

The expansion of the church was phenomenal. Who would have known that the Moondog Corporation would have built their corporate headquarters here? In Zippy, New Jersey. Now, the small town exploded and with that growth, the church expanded, too. At first, Pastor Whorneout enjoyed it. First, a larger sanctuary, then an education wing, then another school building, then a gym and fellowship hall with a full-sized kitchen. Then the Christian school. Kindergarten to grade twelve.

And along came the headaches and stress.

Pastor Whorneout had been with the church for over forty years, and now he was tired, grumpy, and had seen it all. Or he thought he had seen it all. Now, the Christian school was starting a baseball team program. Building a small ballpark right about where the dairy farmer's barn once sat on the land.

Tonight was the meeting to choose the name of the baseball team. The baseball team committee meeting. Pastor Whorneout was looking forward to this as much as he looked forward to listening to his parishioners' comment on his sermons. Another meeting consisting of church lay leaders, money families, descendants of charter members of the church, and every single one will have a different opinion. The only meeting that he could envision that was worse than this one might be was the Christmas wreath committee.

In a bountiful stroke of logic, Pastor Whorneout suggested that since the school's basketball team, the volleyball team, the checkers team, the chess team, the bowling team, the lacrosse team, the football team, and the knitting team, were all called the "Saints" that this meeting could be a waste of time, but, no, it is not that easy!

Wednesday evening. Eight o'clock. In the basement conference room. The meeting began. Pastor Whorneout scanned the room and noticed all the same arguers . . . or rather, ah, attendees.

He opened with a prayer.

In a tired voice, Pastor Whorneout prayed, "Lord, please guide us and bless us with wisdom. . .."

Mr. Pho-Fum raised his hand first. Pastor Whorneout knew he would. He always does. Mr. Pho-Fum was very zealous in the church business. He was about forty years old, owned a liquor distribution warehouse business in town, was very short, and had a bad combover. He also spoke his words with a whistle. He had a few gaps in his teeth. He and Mrs. Pho-Fum picked very original names for their children.

Fee, Fi, and Larry.

Pastor Whorneout called on him right away. Might as well face the music right away.

Off he went, in an endless whistle of words.

"Thank you, Pastor Whorneout. I have been thinking about this for months! I made some notes. So excited! I love baseball! Here are my ideas for heavenly baseball and geography baseball!"

Most of the attendees groaned. Pastor Whorneout buckled his seat belt to prevent falling out of his chair.

With about seventy-two pages of notes spread out on the table in front of him, Mr. Pho-Fum began.

"Page one. I suggest the name of the team be The Saints. But we will also rename important parts of the game, and our team to represent our beliefs! Home plate in our new ballpark will be the collection plate. Our coaches will be pastors, and relief pitchers are angels!"

Pastor Whorneout groaned and leaned forward and rested his head on his heads, with his elbows on the table. Mr. Snickerdoodle did the same thing.

Nothing stopped, Mr. Pho-Fum. Commence whistling words.

"Page two. Hitting a homer is going to Heaven. The seats, way out in the outfields, are not the bleachers. They are Hell! Get it? Hot blazing sun. Relentless! The umpires are the Sanhedrin. Errors in the field are sins. Safe on base is a blessing. Making an out invokes automatic forgiveness. Striking out with the bases loaded or hitting into a double play requires repentance. The dugouts are the choir lofts, the young ballplayers, our student athletes are disciples and apostles. The area just beyond the outfield fences is the Promised Land and foul territory in left field is. . .."

That was all he could take. Pastor Whorneout unbuckled his seat belt; he stood up and shouted. He waved his arms in the air.

"Enough! I have had it! Over! My goodness! For the love of Saint Peter! The name of the baseball team is The Saints. All those in favor say, aye."

Every single committee member, including Mr. Pho-Fum, raised their hands and said, "Aye."

"Any nays?" Pastor Whorneout asked with bulging eyeballs, as he scanned the table, while daring any further words or discussion.

No one dared to say a word or object.

"Seeing none. It is a done deal. Fold your hands. We will now pray. Praise the Lord. Amen. The team name is The Saints. Meeting adjourned. Good night!"

Everyone rose and began to shuffle out of the room in silence. Mrs. Wobblebutt quickly wobbled over to Mr. Pho-Fum, who had his seventy-two pages of notes under his arm and was slowly walking out of the room. Her curiosity had the best of her.

"Mr. Pho-Fum, thank you. I am a baseball lover, too. I rather enjoyed your ideas for heavenly baseball. I want to know what the names for foul territory are. But first, let me guess, the left field side is Sodom and right field side is Gomorrah."

Mr. Pho-Fum looked up and said, "Thank you, Mrs. Wobblebutt. Ah, no. Right field is Paterson and the left field is Newark. I was moving onto the geography section when Pastor Whorneout lost his mind. I was up to page three."

The next morning, Pastor Guggenheim Whorneout called the bishop of his district.

He did not hesitate one second when he heard the bishop answer the phone.

"Bishop Washboard, I want to put my retirement papers in. Effective, hopefully, and prayerfully, before baseball season begins."

Spark

Stranger

"Henry forlornly emerged from his basement man cave after his football team lost the last game of the football season. The season was over. No playoffs this year. Again. This was now fourteen years in a row, with no qualification for the playoffs. He opened the basement door and stepped into the kitchen, and Woofy, the family dog, met him at the top of the stairs. Woofy growled, barked, and snarled at Henry."

"Woofy! Stop! It is me, boy! Don't you recognize me?"

Spark

In A Post, Now Deleted

"In a post, now deleted on the Blabber social media site, Executive Vice President of Overseas Sales for the Mega-Corporation, Mr. Wally Walker, strongly suggested that some type of foreign nefarious coercion was behind his department's stunning defeat in the potato sack race at the company picnic."

18

Flash!

Calling in the Cats

Hot summer nights have a way of melting your soul. Cold winter nights have a way of freezing your soul. Fall nights tease you by freezing you and warming you. Spring nights do the same.

It was October. The morning was cold. The afternoon was warm. Now it was cold.

The cats were outside cats. Generally, they stayed outside no matter what the weather. They had strategic places to hide. They were cats.

They only returned home to sleep, eat, and rest for a while before returning to their domain.

To do what it is that cats do.

The note that was sitting on the kitchen table was brief. Just a few words. He found it when his work shift was over. A ten-hour shift. His wife did not work. He was the sole bread-winner in the house.

She wrote the note in pencil on plain white paper. He picked it up and read it. Her perfume lingered on it. No question that he could smell it. Even without lifting the paper up to his senses. The pencil she used in composing the note sat on the table next to where she left the note. The tip of the pencil had been sharp; now, the lead tip had a flat edge to it.

"I do not know what to write other than I have left for

good. This has been coming for a very long time. You knew it. I knew it. Good bye."

She signed it with a single letter. "L"

His wife's name was Laura.

He gently replaced the paper on the kitchen table. Where he found it.

A few short steps to the cupboard. Where he kept the whiskey.

He took the bottle of his favorite blend and poured three fingers into a whiskey glass.

The first sip burned. The second sip burned less. The last sip had no burn at all.

Now the whiskey glass sat rather properly on the kitchen table.

Right next to the note.

He opened the back door of their home and called in the cats. They came running across the lawn. In the fading light, he could see them. They were hungry. They were cold.

Time to feed them. Time for rest.

Her perfume lingered, even though she was no longer here. Gone. It would linger long after she was gone. He knew it.

He almost wondered why she had perfume on, except he knew the answer. She was meeting him.

If he could cry, then he would do so. But he could not cry. Sometimes, tears are not worth the effort.

He almost picked the note up again to smell her perfume. Instead, he went back to the cupboards. First, he would feed the cats. They loved him in their own feline ways. The two of them lingered at his feet.

Feed the cats.

Then the whiskey.

The whiskey would mask her perfume. In one way or another.

Hot summer nights have a way of melting your soul. Cold winter nights have a way of freezing your soul. Fall nights tease you by freezing you and warming you. Spring nights do the same.

It was October. The morning was cold. The afternoon was warm. Now it was cold.

Very cold.

He was glad that he called the cats in for the night.

It was too cold outside tonight.

For the cats.

For him, too.

Spark

Heaven

"There are familiar songs that the angels play in Heaven. They are the songs within your heart."

Spark

Help Wanted

"A help wanted job advertisement in the local newspaper:

Edmundo's roller-skating factory is seeking a full-time roller-skate tester. Must have own medical insurance, good balance, and the ability to bounce right back up after failure. A good sense of humor, a large backside, and no teeth are a plus."

Spark

Clueless

"It was deeply disappointing when after a largely unsuccessful thirty-two-year career on the police force, Police Detective Nimrod Clueless finally realized what his family's last name actually meant."

Spark

Memory

"My primary care physician recommended that I make an appointment to see a neurologist. But for the life of me, I cannot remember why."

ABOUT THE AUTHOR

If you ask Paul John Hausleben, he will tell you that he is not an author, he is just a storyteller. His mission is to continue to write and tell stories to warm your heart, make you laugh, make you think, and sometimes make you cry, just a little. Most of all, he deals in memories, and helps you to remember the good times of your own life, and the special people who touched you along the way. He displays amazing versatility in his writing by covering a wide variety of genres.

Paul was born and raised in Paterson, and then nearby Haledon, New Jersey, and began writing at an early age. He revisited a writing career later in his life, and he now is the author of several novels, compilations, short stories, music reviews, and audio and video works. Most of his work touches upon nostalgic remembrances of simpler times, and tells the stories of heartfelt, humorous, and special human relationships. Mr. Hausleben is the owner, and the driving creative force of God Bless the Keg Publishing LLC. Paul is a skilled and award-winning photographer, and his publishing company features much of his photographic work. Other than writing and photography, among many careers both paid and unpaid, he is a former semi-professional hockey goaltender, a music fan and music reviewer, and an avid ice hockey, American football, football, and overall sports fan, and a former military radio operator.

He is a supporter of the Nottingham Forest Football Club.

Mr. Hausleben is an avid amateur radio operator. He holds an extra class amateur radio license with the call letters WA2ASQ. Paul is a Morse code and digital mode operator and he enjoys on-the-air radio contests and chasing long distance (DX) stations from all over the world while using very low power (QRP) transmissions to do so.

Mr. Paul John Hausleben now resides in Somewhere, U.S.A., but his heart always remains along Belmont Avenue in good old Paterson, and Haledon, New Jersey.

A Somewhat Correct Answer

G: All of the above, except for selection D. D is for ding-dongs.

Other Work by Mr. Paul John Hausleben

The Time Bomb in The Cupboard and Other Adventures of Harry and Paul

The Night Always Comes, Another story from the Adventures of Harry and Paul

Reunion, A sequel to the Night Always Comes and Another story from the Adventures of Harry and Paul

The Miracle Tree, Another story from the Adventures of Harry and Paul

The Chronicles of Henson

Heaven's Gain

The Final Adventure of Harry and Paul

Geyer Street Gardens

Beneath the Mask of a Hockey Goaltender

Another story from the Adventures of Harry and Paul

Where the River Bends and Curls

Tales of the Quiet Stranger in the Black Hat

Crows on a High Wire

A Bowl Full of Marbles

A New Jersey Christmas Tale

Christmas Cocktails

Flashes, Spark, and Shorts: Flash One and Flash Two and Three and Four

Experiences: A Series of Essays on My Life

The Many Cases of Detective Lyle Odell

And a few others too!

Mr. Paul John Hausleben
(Age unknown. Best guess is very old)

You may write to the author at ctte27@gmail.com

Published by God Bless the Keg Publishing LLC

Henrico, Virginia, U.S.A.

You may write to the publisher at
Godblessthekegpublishing@gmail.com

"Life's simple pleasures are so often the best ones!"

Follow Paul John Hausleben on Facebook and enjoy samples of his photography, receive updates on new releases, and enjoy his general meanderings. Book reviews are important to authors and publishers! Please consider leaving a book review for this publication on your favorite book website, blog, or publication. Thank you.

www.ingramcontent.com/pod-product-compliance
Lightning Source LLC
LaVergne TN
LVHW020714110826
845149LV00012B/2264

* 9 7 9 8 9 8 9 4 4 9 0 4 0 *